CW01628711

SCREWING MR. SCROOGE

NICHOLE GREENE

Cover by Opulent Designs and Swag

Created with Vellum

For all the readers like me who love holiday movies but wish they were spicier.

Ho Ho Ho, bitches.

CONTENT WARNING

There are brief mentions of addiction, overdose, parental loss, sex work, foster care, and child neglect in this book.

CHAPTER 1

CLARA

THERE ARE two types of people in the world. The always on time, chronically stressed, sticks in the mud are the first. I'm currently surrounded by a swarm of them, all hurrying through the rain in their black and gray suits, umbrellas knocking against each other as they hustle toward their cubicles of despair. Then there are the wild cards, the go with flow and live life on your own terms type. That's me.

My bright orange skirt over spider web leggings paired with a black cat sweater stand out on the River Walk like a sore thumb. The yellow umbrella I've had since college kicked the bucket while I waited for the L in my neighborhood on the south side of the city. Fine with me because it might be a drizzly, gray late October day in the Windy City but it's still above fifty degrees and that deserves a celebration.

I walk up the stairs and into the building that houses the temp agency I work for. Being called in specifically for a meeting with the woman I'd be filling in for has never happened to me before. A strange request, but she said it was absolutely necessary, so who am I to question it?

The suits on the elevator all give me the side eye. They obviously aren't used to this much in-your-face style. It's okay, I'm an acquired taste. I give them a sweet smile as I step off the elevator.

Tillie, the receptionist, is sitting behind her desk as I walk into the lobby. She stands to greet me and waves me back toward one of the conference rooms. "Mrs. Preston is already back there waiting for you. Good luck." She gives me a warm smile before she sits and calls another person back.

Taking a deep breath, I push the door open to find a very pregnant woman sitting at one end of a conference table with four binders spread out before her. She stands, dressed in a slim fitting black dress and jacket. Her hair is pulled back in a sleek low bun and her makeup subtle and understated. Her brown eyes move from my face down to my shoes.

"Clara Snow?" she asks with raised brows.

"That's me." I hold my hand out and give hers a firm shake.

"Nice to meet you. Sara Preston." She gestures the chair

across from her. "Have a seat. There's a lot to go over before you start tomorrow."

I sit down, glancing at the titles on the binders.

Company Procedures and Expectations

Mr. Bennett's Daily Schedule

Mr. Bennett's Expectations

Everything Else You Might Not Expect But Need to Know

Holy fucking shit. Who is this guy? Forget stick in the mud, more like stick up the ass.

"I can see you're already overwhelmed," she says with a slight grimace. "Your references were impeccable. I chose you from a pool of hundreds. I have no doubt you can do this."

I look up at her from the binder in front of me. "I never met a challenge I couldn't hurdle. I'm guessing Mr. Bennett has high and firm expectations?"

"He does." She nods. "But he's a good and fair boss. If you show up every day and do your job well, you'll have no issues with him. Shall we get started?"

An hour and a half later, and my eyes are crossing with the immense amount of information I'm taking in. I know everything about TechJet from the founding to the company ethos to the structure of the meetings I'll be expected to take notes during. And when it comes to Asher Bennett, I know everything from his preferred breakfast, either steel cut oats or an egg white and spinach omelet with fresh orange juice and black coffee, to where he prefers his dry cleaning is sent. The man has a rigid schedule that, according to my new bestie Sara, never deviates.

We take a break and order sandwiches from the deli across the street. As we're waiting, I notice she's kicked off her heels and is rubbing her feet. Relief crosses her face as she works tension out of her arches.

"When are you due?" I ask.

"I'm being induced tomorrow at five p.m." She relaxes back into her chair. "Any questions beyond what we've discussed so far?"

"What's the company culture like? And the other big wigs?"

"Good question." She smiles over at me. "It's pretty relaxed, despite what I'm going over with you. Nico Mattia is our in-house corporate counsel and very laid back. Don't be surprised if he rides a skateboard through the office. He's absolutely ruthless in a courtroom, though."

Interesting. Definitely seems like the opposite of Mr. Bennett.

"Stella James is the CFO. She's serious and smart as a whip. She's a girl's girl, though, so anything you need, go to her first." She talks about a few others who are high up on the ladder but won't be around as often. "The office culture is also, shockingly, casual. There's a break room with video games, a pool table, and lounge area. A full gym with an on-staff trainer. As with most tech companies, dress code is business casual, but I take my cues from Mr. Bennett and always dress business professional. He'll be fine if you want to personalize your desk. Bring in family photos or anything like that."

I won't be bringing in family photos, but I can personalize my space. Especially with the holidays coming up. Christmas is my absolute favorite time of year.

The sandwiches arrive, and we spend lunch time getting to know the basics about each other. We won't be working together but having basic knowledge of Sara and how she approaches her work will help me assimilate into the role. Especially with such rigid exceptions from Mr. Bennett.

There are no pictures of him, but in my mind, he's graying with a pot belly and ear hair. Maybe even occasional pit stains and pepper in his teeth. Based off the binder of rules I've had to memorize today; he can't be younger than fifty.

I live in a lively neighborhood, four blocks from Chicago Midway Airport and about four feet from the Orange Line. The Mexican restaurant on the ground floor of the building my studio is in is always busy. The pork tacos are great, and the margaritas are even better.

Nothing beats the company of my fuzzy, black void, Steve, though. Coming home after a long day of peopling to his casual indifference makes my heart go pitter patter. His tail swipes back and forth as he sits on the window ledge, probably plotting world domination.

I set my bag down and walk over to him, scratching behind his left ear in greeting. It's a weird ritual, but it's one of the only places he tolerates being touched. I found him dumpster diving a couple years ago and decided to bring him home, at least for a flea dip. I left the door open one day, an invitation for him to leave, but he just sat on the windowsill and watched until I closed the door. He and I have been filling this studio apartment ever since.

Sara let me keep the binders to look through before I start tomorrow. It's a little weird to be starting a job on a Friday, even as a temp, but I'm rolling with it. I pour a glass of wine and heat up my leftovers from last night, settling in to listen to some classic folk rock and study up on my new boss.

Asher Bennett has a mile-long list of dislikes, ranging from sugar in his coffee to the color yellow. What kind of curmudgeon doesn't like yellow? Is this guy part troll?

I finish my wine and wash my lone wine glass in the sink that serves as both my bathroom and kitchen sink. Tomorrow is Halloween, so I pull out my favorite sweater and skirt, both of which are the colors of Halloween but muted without over-the-top prints. As much as I'd love to wear my witch dress, I'm guessing that would be too much for Mr. Bennett. Don't want to send him into cardiac arrest with too much personality right off the bat.

I've just turned off the light when my phone lights up with a text from Daniel, the manager at the homeless shelter I volunteer at on the weekends.

Daniel: Sorry for the late text but I need a favor
Clara: Sure, anything
Daniel: We're trying to secure enough funds to buy the other half of the block

I'm not sure what I can do to help with that, there are some months I live off ramen and Easy Mac.

Daniel: We also need the zoning committee to grant us permission to purchase
Clara: Okay...
Daniel: I wanted to know if you would go to them.
Daniel: Use that MBA you have from Northwestern
Daniel: You'll add credibility

It's a no-brainer for me to say yes. I've been volunteering there since I was a freshman in college and searching for meaning in my life outside academia.

Clara: Of course, I'll help in any way I can. When will you meet with them?
Daniel: I'm not sure, the committeeman is hard to pin down.

Clara: I have a temp job through January, but I'm sure I can make something work

Daniel: Great, we'll talk more this weekend

CHAPTER 2

ASHER

SIX HOURS into Sara going on maternity leave, and things have already gone to hell. I've not even stepped into the office, and I'm fielding calls and emails from interested overseas investors. I've built TechJet incredibly fast and successfully from the ground up, but we're about to hit the ceiling on growth capacity unless I get another influx of capital.

While I was taking a call from London and waiting for my driver, a cab drove by splashing my pants with cold, slushy street water and ruining the suit which undoubtedly cost more than his piece-of-shit sedan. We have a morning round up at nine this morning, so I don't have time to go back up to my condo and change. I hope the new temp catches on quick because she's being pushed into the deep end, and I don't have time to play lifeguard.

By the time I walk through the door, there's a steady stream of employees arriving. As is the norm with most tech startups we have foregone the old model of corporate culture and cubicles shifting to a co-working environment with comfortable seating and stimulating art. Over half my employees work remotely. The state-of-the-art building is four levels, the first is a lobby, cafe, and in-house gym. The second and third are workspaces for development, design, and engineering. The eastern and southern facing walls are floor to ceiling windows, highlighting the gloomy, autumn sky this morning. The fourth level has the executive suites. We each have a closed office with a central lounge. Our executive assistants' desks are clustered together in that room.

For as laid back as the atmosphere we have cultivated is, most of the employees look down and scurry out of my way as soon as I enter the building. It's not that I try to be an asshole, it's just who I am. The pressure of my employee's lives weighs heavily on me. Plus, the drive to give the metaphorical finger to my father is always there.

I started this company with my two best friends from prep school. Nico and Stella have been beside me for over twenty years. We barely manage weekends apart at this point.

Taylor, Stella's assistant, is already at his desk deep in a pile of paperwork. I stop by his desk and tap my knuckle on it. "Can you send a floral arrangement to the hospital for Sara?"

"I already did. One from you and one from the entire

office," he answers with an easy smile. One of the only employees confident enough to hold eye contact with me.

"Good man. I should have stolen you away from Stella while Sara is gone."

"Not if you wanted to live another day," Stella says as she emerges from her office. "Oh my god, what happened to your suit?"

"Cab splashed me."

"I think Nico has an extra suit in his office. You should be able to fit." She disappears into his office and comes out a moment later with a burgundy Brioni suit. "I know you're color adverse but it's better than that," she glances down at my leg in obvious disgust. "Your shirt and tie will work with it, too."

"Fuck," I grumble as I walk back into my office, hitting the button to turn the glass from clear to opaque. "Tell my temp to see me as soon as she gets in," I say as I close the door behind me.

My phone rings with a text notification from my mother.

Mom: We need to know your plus one for the charity gala in Paris
Asher: I'm not bringing one
Mom: I'll find someone
Asher: No.
Mom: You can't show up alone
Asher: Watch me

Mom: Ash, I'll find some possible dates and you can choose

I won't be choosing any of them, but I won't be telling her that. It should be easy enough to find reasons to say no. I don't have time to entertain high maintenance women, even just a for a night. The company is in the middle of a high stakes time, I can't risk distractions.

Asher: Fine
Mom: I love you
Asher: Love you, too

I strip off my jacket and toss it on the chair opposite my desk. My belt and pants quickly follow. I'm bent over, ass to the door when I hear it swing open. I stand quickly, one leg in and one leg out, and my eyes lock on an unfamiliar face.

Big, gray eyes rounded in shock, long brown hair, parted pink lips, and cheeks that are rapidly turning scarlet with embarrassment. She's fucking gorgeous. That thought has no place in this moment, but I can't bat it away.

"Get out," I bark.

"S-sorry," she stammers as she turns and closes the door behind her.

Her ass, holy fuck. It's perfection.

Snap out of it.

Please, don't let her be my new temp. The thought echoes through my mind like a silent prayer. I don't need this; a massively embarrassing moment before I've even learned her name.

I take a deep breath once I'm dressed before going out to greet her. My hand is clammy as I reach for the doorknob, so I brush it against my thigh. It must be the embarrassment getting to me. Literally caught with my pants down.

Fucking hell.

I purposefully ignore Stella and Taylor, choosing instead to focus on the woman sitting at Sara's desk and setting out a few personal items. Her hair is a shiny, chestnut curtain cascading down her back. She's wearing a black leather skirt, knee length and a burnt orange sweater with black cat-eyeglasses.

When she finally raises her head to look at me, I can see the mortification written all over her face. Good, that makes two of us. She hurries to her feet quickly, holding out her hand. I don't take it.

"Hi, sir. Mr. Bennett." She pushes the glasses up her nose. "I'm Clara Snow, your temp."

More like temptress.

"I'm so sorry for that," she gestures at the open office door. "They told me to go right in, I should have knocked."

"Anyone with common sense would have," I snap. I should feel bad when she flinches at my harsh tone, but I just don't have it in me to be contrite.

"We just relayed your message." Stella raises a brow at me. "We didn't realize it was going to take you ten minutes to change clothes. Or that you'd leave the door unlocked."

She looks like she's barely holding her laughter in. I can tell by the crinkle in the corner of her eyes.

"Where's Nico?" I look into his still dark office.

"On his way, sir." Tory, his assistant, wrings her hands. "He said he might be a minute or two late for the round up."

I check my watch and clench my jaw. Irritated with fucking everybody. Could this day get any worse?

"I laid my suit out in my office," I look down at the temp. "You'll need to take it to the dry cleaners. Hopefully they can salvage it."

"Okay." She stands and moves toward my office.

I hold a hand out. "After the round up," I say through gritted teeth. The disapproving look Stella throws my way has me wanting to escape the walls closing in on me feeling. I stalk over to the stairwell and take them two at a time down to the second level lounge where we have our weekly meeting.

I need to calm the fuck down before the meeting. I scare most of my employees on a good day, and today is a day crafted by the demons in the seventh level of hell. My jaw aches with the force I'm exerting on it as I breathe in a few deep breaths, trying, and failing, to calm down.

Stella's heels click on the metal of the stairs as her nails tap on the railing. She gives me the same look from earlier but with more teeth. She wouldn't fully call me out in front of our assistants but she's about to hand me my ass now.

"What the actual fuck is your problem?" she asks as she comes to a halt beside me.

"An amalgamation of shit topped off by the fact that my new assistant just literally caught me with my pants down."

"Not her fault," she smirks. "Also, it's not like there aren't hundreds of people who have seen your naked ass."

"She could file harassment charges and probably fucking win."

She scoffs. "You should have seen her face. She was horrified. She won't be filing anything. Although if you don't tone down the rage, she might just walk out. And I wouldn't blame her."

Sara and I painstakingly went through round after round of resumes. I know what's waiting out there for me, and it isn't good. Clara's was far and away the biggest standout.

"Half the employees are going to piss their pants if you walk into that meeting with that look on your face." She circles her finger in my face. "And you look like Barney in that purple suit."

A huff of frustrated laughter comes from my chest. "I was thinking more like Twilight Sparkle."

"I see your nieces have molded you into a bronie." She opens the door and strolls through first.

"What can I say? They're persuasive."

The hint of a smile that was on my face falls as Taylor leads Clara off the elevator with a hand on the small of her back. It's not an inappropriate placement, more comforting than anything, and yet a bitter weight settles inside me. I don't know where this is coming from, but it needs to be squashed immediately.

CHAPTER 3

CLARA

ASHER BENNETT IS DEFINITELY NOT a middle-aged troll like I was expecting. He's worse. A cruel, harsh man packaged in the body of Roman god. The only thing I saw when I walked in on him changing were muscled thighs with a smattering of dark hair. The kind of thighs that could crack a watermelon.

He commands the room as he walks in front of a white board, jotting down ideas and sharing numbers that honestly mean nothing to me. Half of the people watch him with stars in their eyes, the other half look like they might vomit. I'm dancing on the line separating the two camps.

His hair is several shades darker than mine and styled to perfection in a way that seems casually pompous. He probably has a set amount of time for his hair, forcing it into submission in three minutes or less. His eyes are a dark and stormy green but maybe that's just because the only time I've been close enough to see the different shades he's been pissed. His jaw is wide and as chiseled as his thighs appeared to be.

Stop thinking about his thighs.

Suddenly everyone in the room turns and looks at me. *Fuck.* I was daydreaming about his thighs. He motions me to stand up impatiently. I stand hesitantly, hating being the center of attention even for small periods of time.

"This is Clara Snow, my temporary assistant. Treat her just as you would Sara."

I wave awkwardly and sit down as soon as his laser-focused eyes leave me. His gaze feels too intense, too hypnotic. Someone asks a question I don't catch, and his response is short and caustic. The perfect reminder I needed that he might be pretty but he's a dick.

He dismisses everyone as he draws the meeting to a close, but I feel the weight of him looking directly at me. I can't bring myself to make eye contact, so I grab the small notebook I brought and turn for the elevator.

"He's not as bad as his first impression was." Stella joins me on the elevator. She's tall and statuesque with a sexy rasp to her voice. Her long blonde hair flows over one shoulder, and her blue eyes sparkle as she hits the button for the top floor.

"Half the people who work here seem to be afraid of him."

"He's all bark and very little bite." The elevator opens

and we walk off together. "Seriously, he's had a terrible morning, he's not usually this bad. You'll see."

"Fingers crossed." I give her a genuine smile, Sara's description of her being a girl's girl rings true. At least I have that going for me. Taylor and Tory are nice as well.

I walk to Mr. Bennett's office and knock, no way in hell will I ever walk in on him again. When there's no answer, I push the door in slowly. Thankfully, he's not back up here yet, so I dart in and grab his suit. The second it's in my arms the scent of his cologne nearly brings me to my knees.

It smells like sex and power wrapped in a ridiculous amount of money. Which makes sense when I glance down and see the Tom Ford label on his suit. Obviously, he's wealthy beyond measure; he's from the Bennett family, of Bennett Development and Construction. It's the single largest developer from Pittsburg to Denver.

I hear his voice from the lounge and scurry out of his office. The less time I spend in here, the better. I memorized the name of the dry cleaner he uses, so I don't have to stop at my desk to pull out one of the binders and cross check.

"Clara," he calls from the door of Stella's office as I hit the button for the elevator. "Do you know where to take my suit?"

"Doughtery and Sons Dry Cleaners," I say with confidence and a sunny smile.

He looks at me silently for an uncomfortably long time and then nods, returning to his conversation with Stella. No smile back, but that's okay. I'll either get one from him someday, or I'll just wither away and die.

It's drizzling as I exit the building. I know I could use the car service for these errands, but the walk is only a few blocks and he's not scheduled in any meetings. It's good to get extra steps in when I can. The L stop is literally right outside my door, so I don't get much exercise walking to and from there. I've never had enough extra cash lying around for a gym membership, either, which is why my body is soft and thick instead of trim and defined.

Carrying his suit in my arms like this is pure torture. Every inhale brings his scent into my nostrils, and fuck if I don't want to bury my face in the soft wool. I'm not a very sexual person, but I can't help but think the dirtiest thoughts of kneeling between his powerful thighs while being immersed in a cloud of his intoxicating scent.

What the hell, Clara?

Maybe I need to be around men to cut out this neediness. I should go out tonight, at the very least sit at the bar after work and have a drink. It's not like I'll get trick or treaters at my apartment.

The rain changed from drizzle to steady to a full on my down pour throughout the day. I forgot to buy a new umbrella so even with the ten feet from the L to my building's front door, I'm soaked. I walk up to my apartment and change from skirt and sweater to jeans and a hoodie before feeding Steve.

He gives me his usual apathetic look as I run my hand

down his soft, black coat. Occasionally I'll catch him in a good mood, and he'll give me a little purr when I do this, but today is not that day. I give him a scratch behind the ears anyway.

I walk downstairs to the restaurant, waving hello to the servers who all know my name. The bar is empty as I take a seat. Maria, the bartender, throws a rag over her shoulder and walks down to me.

"The usual?" she asks as she slides a coaster to me.

"Yeah, on the rocks tonight."

"Pork tacos?"

"Yes, please. I'll take three."

She strolls away to put my order into the computer and brings me a bowl of salsa and a basket of chips. "How was your day?"

"Good." I dip a chip into the salsa. "I started a new job today," I say before biting into the chip, loving the spicy tang of the salsa on my tongue.

"Where at this time?" she asks as she makes my margarita.

"TechJet."

"Oh, the CEO of that company is hot," she says as fans herself.

No shit. And I saw him in his underwear.

"He's also an absolute ass." I take a drink, savoring the bite of the tequila. This was the best idea.

"Did you meet him?"

"I did." I signed a standard NDA; I know I could tell her my position, but Maria is nosey. I don't want her pushing me for insider information, even innocently. "How do you know about him?"

She tilts her head and looks at me quizzically. "He's one of the city's most eligible bachelors. I thought everyone knew about him."

I shrug and eat another chip. "I don't pay attention to that stuff."

"You should. He's single." She wiggles her brows.

Least surprising thing I've heard from her. With his personality I wouldn't be surprised if he's never gotten laid. Maybe he needs to, might make him easier going. But one thing is certain, I won't be the one to fill that role.

CHAPTER 4

ASHER

"WHAT DO you think about the new temp?" Nico asks as he sits back on my couch, a cold beer in hand. He and Stella come over for every away game the Bears play. My family has a box at Soldier Field so we're always there for home games.

"It's only been one day. I haven't given it much thought."

That's total bullshit.

I've been thinking about her for what feels like every fucking other minute since she strode into my office while Nico's pants were around my ankles. The most inappropriate thought being wondering if the shocked 'o' her lips formed is like the face she makes when she comes.

I take a pull from the bottle of beer cradled in my hands

and hope to fuck my life long best friends are too busy tripping over each other to notice me. It's been years already, and I need them to just take the leap and admit they have feelings for each other. Stella won't because she thinks Nico wouldn't want her. Nico is just an idiot. I love them both, but I can't take much more of their unrequited love and longing looks.

"I think you've given Clara more thought than you're letting on," Stella says from her spot across from us. "Every time she'd walk by, your eyes would follow."

Yeah, because she's gorgeous in the most unexpected way. Those big gray eyes that show every emotion instantly pulled me in. But I'm her boss, so I'm not thinking about her like that.

"Our walls are glass; any movement pulls the eye."

"Bullshit," Nico says with a snort. "I could be on fire, and you wouldn't notice."

Luckily the game starts, and we direct all our attention to the second half kickoff. The Bears end up losing, and we drown our sorrows with deep dish and more beer. We talk about everything but business for a couple more hours, another ritual we started years ago. Sundays are for fun.

I walk Stella and Nico out of my penthouse, turning as the private elevator doors close to survey the view from my living room windows. My building sits near the Chicago River with a view of Lake Michigan on one side and the city on the other. It's a beautiful space, but my mother wants me to buy a home near them out in the suburbs. I can't bring myself to do it, because as much as this space feels empty, a sprawling suburban estate would feel even more so.

I pick up the bottles and dishes in the living room even though my maid service will be here tomorrow. I can't stand waking up to messes. Some would describe me as rigid; I just prefer things organized.

Speaking of organization, I need to check my calendar for the week and make sure Clara added all the new appointments before she left on Friday. Taylor and Tori did a great job of easing her into the way I like things done.

I did, however, notice that Taylor was giving her a lot of extra attention. Much more than necessary, and I swear I caught him looking at her ass once or twice. I'll have to put a stop to that. For business liability reasons, obviously.

The last thing TechJet needs when we're so close to punching a hole through the market is a lawsuit. Which is why I need to quit thinking about her outside of her role in my professional life. Easier said than done because as I look down at the lights below me, I can't help but wonder if she's out there.

Where does she live?

Is she in a relationship?

That one gives me pause. Maybe she's got a long-term boyfriend. That'd put an end to my curiosity.

Maybe.

No, definitely. Irritated with myself, I turn off the lights in my living room and walk down the hall to my bedroom. I flip the shower on and strip, dumping my clothes in the appropriate bins, my jeans in the dark clothing bin, my shirt and undershirt in the whites, and my underwear and socks in the delicate bin.

The process of cleaning myself helps distract me from my thoughts of Clara until I smell my body wash. Immediately I recall the way she dropped her face into my suit jacket and sniffed it. Her whole body relaxed, like my scent soothed her or something. She had no idea I was watching from the lounge.

Fuck, that was hot. I wonder if she'd melt into my arms like that. Her lush body pressed against the hard lines of my own. My fingers sliding along the length of her silky strands. Her fist wrapped around my cock, pumping me slowly and firmly.

When I look down my body, I see my own hand wrapped around my dick. I try to talk myself out of it, but I throb in my own hand as I envision her. The way she walked back into the office, smelling of the rain drops gathered in her hair and wetting her sweater.

What was she wearing under those clothes? I slide my hand up and down my length, squeezing as I do. Is she a lace girl? Satin? Is she practical and wears cotton? My pace increases at the thought of her wearing cotton with half her ass cheeks hanging out.

Fuck.

This is so wrong. I feel like I'm violating her just thinking about this. But then I imagine her bent over my desk, her skirt pushed up to her waist as she writes notes for me. I bet she'd be so pretty and wet for me while I tease her.

My breaths come quicker and harsher as I work my

cock. All the time picturing my new assistant in the dirtiest positions, with me cumming all over her ass. I rest my forehead against the marble of my shower wall as my cock jerks in my hand, releasing all over it.

How am I supposed to face her tomorrow morning knowing I just came picturing her ass coated in my cum?

CHAPTER 5

CLARA

"GOOD MORNING," I greet Taylor with a bright smile as we walk into the building together.

"You're too energetic this early in the morning on a Monday." He sips his coffee and holds the door open for me. "And what's in the box?"

"Decorations." I shift the box in my arms as I step onto the elevator. "Sara said I was welcome to decorate and personalize her desk while I'm here so that's what I'm doing."

"Family photos?" He asks, peering over the top.

"No, holiday decor."

"Gotcha," he says, nodding.

"Long weekend?" I ask.

"My college buddies came in for the weekend. We went to a Bears watch party."

"Ah," I say with a knowing grin. "I don't know much about basketball."

He does a double take. "The Bears are a football team. Are you not from Chicago?"

"Whoops," I drop the box on my desk, noting that Mr. Bennett is already in his office. "I'm clearly not a sports person." I make a big show of pulling decor out, not wanting to get into my background.

It's one of the reasons I like working for a temp agency. The constant change of jobs, location, and co-workers has always appealed to me. Stability is so foreign to me that anything remotely close to routine makes me squirmy. It's one of the reasons the agency keeps me at the top of their list for big clients: I thrive with the fluidity of the jobs.

I pull a roll of evergreen garland from my box and lay it across the front of my desk. Then I pull out the tabletop tree I found at Goodwill this weekend. I finish emptying out the box when I feel his presence behind me. I glance down at my phone, worried I missed his breakfast, but I still have plenty of time.

"What are you doing?" Even his voice sounds rich, the voice that can command a room or tear you down to nothing.

"Good morning." I give him my most professional smile, trying and failing to hold his gaze. "Sara said I could decorate my desk."

"It's November third." He looks at the tree and garland pointedly.

"Yes." I nod.

"Thanksgiving comes before Christmas." His sleeves are already rolled up to his elbows. I glance at his watch—since when did a man wearing a watch become sexy?

"Last I checked, yes." I keep the same sweet smile locked on my face. Something about this man makes me want to sass.

"So why are you decorating for Christmas already?" A red flush is creeping up his neck as he towers over me. I'll have to stop wearing flats.

"Ash," Stella says from her office. "I need you in here."

His jaw ticks as he gives me one more disapproving look before stalking across the lounge to her office. I grimace across the way to Taylor who shrugs. I pull up the app to order Mr. Bennett's breakfast and then go back to my decor when I get a notification from the internal messaging system from Taylor.

Taylor: He's always like that. Don't let it stop you.
Clara: Now I see why everyone is terrified of him.
Clara: So grumpy. What a Scrooge.

Taylor chuckles as he reads my message but stops as soon as Mr. Scrooge exits Stella's office. He stops in front of my desk. His scent surrounding me while he looks down at the progress I'm making. The distaste is clearly written on his stupidly handsome face, but I hit him with my smile once again.

Those deep green eyes lock on mine. "We have to go to New York for the day on Thursday, clear my schedule."

"You and Stella, sir?"

"No, you and I are going." He glances at his watch and then back at me. "Just a day trip."

"Okay," I say, hoping he misses the hesitation. I've never set foot on an airplane.

I grew up in Oklahoma and, as soon as I aged out of the foster system, jumped on a train to Chicago for college. In all my life I only had one adult who every thought I'd amount to anything, the guidance counselor from my high school. She encouraged me to apply for college scholarships, and somehow I ended up with a full ride to Northwestern.

"Is my breakfast on the way?"

"Yes, sir. Do I need to make travel arrangements for us?"

He pauses and looks at me puzzled. "No, we'll take the corporate jet. Did Sara not mention that this could be a possibility?"

"She may have," I say with a grimace. "But there were large binders of information to go over in only a few hours' time. I didn't realize travel would be required."

"Is that a problem?" he asks in a surprisingly gentle tone.

"No, sir." I glance down at my phone seeing the

delivery driver is down in the lobby. "Your breakfast is here," I say, standing.

He frowns at me as I brush past him. I feel the heat radiating off him as my arm grazes his chest. God forbid he move so I can squeeze by without physical contact. The weight of his steely gaze follows me until I look up, making eye contact with him as the elevator doors close.

The next several days go by in a similar manner. I continue to slowly decorate the area around my desk. He keeps sending the disgusted looks, both to my holiday-themed outfits and cheerfully decorated space. But, intermingled, are looks laced with curiosity. I've opened up a bit to Taylor and more to Stella. Something about her puts me at ease, maybe a kindred spirit.

I'm turning off the lamp at my desk, about to walk out into the rainy Chicago night, when Mr. Scrooge steps into to doorway of his office.

"Leaving for the night?" he asks, leaning casually against the doorjamb. He lost his tie and unbuttoned the top two buttons of his shirt after his last meeting of the day. It's irritating how attractive this grumpy man can be when he loosens up a bit.

"Yes, do you want me to order dinner for you before I leave?"

"No," he says as he scratches his jaw. "Thank you, though. I have leftovers from lunch that I can heat up if I stop before I go home. I'll be by at six tomorrow morning to pick you up. Text me your address."

"Oh, you don't have to do that. I can take a cab."

"Don't be ridiculous, the cab fare from the city to Chicago Exec would be expensive."

"Oh," I guess it does make sense that he'd be flying from a smaller airport instead of one of the two majors. I open my phone and send him my address. "I'll see you first thing, I guess. Good night, sir."

"Night."

Once again, he stays propped in the door, watching me until the elevator doors close and I can breathe again.

CHAPTER 6

ASHER

THE MUSCLES in my jaw ache with tension as we pull up in front of a rundown row of buildings several blocks from Midway. Even from inside the town car I can hear the rattle of the L zooming past while we wait for Clara. Some of the shops look operational, but others have plywood over the windows. I never would have expected her to live in a place like this.

A door with bars over the window opens, and she walks out onto the dimly lit sidewalk. As soon as her eyes land on the car, she begins to move toward us. She's wearing a long trench coat, and her legs, what I can see of them, are covered in black stockings.

Thank fuck she's not wearing her weird holiday clothes.

"I'll open the door for her," I say to Tom, my driver, before he unbuckles.

I push the door open and exit the car, holding the door open as she joins me. Her gaze moves over me with the slightest bit of heat mixed with surprise. I can never tell what she's thinking. It drives me up the wall.

"You didn't have to get out to let me in." She sidesteps me and slides across the seat.

"You could just say, 'thank you, Asher.'"

Her orange and vanilla scent fills the cabin of the car. It's such a unique combination, somehow perfectly fits who she is. She's this bizarre enigma of a woman who I, for some inexplicable reason, cannot stop thinking about.

"Thank you, Mr. Bennett," she says with a syrupy sweet tone.

"You can call me Asher."

"Sara told me you prefer Mr. Bennett."

"Sara prefers that." I don't know why she's insisted on calling me that for the past several years. I know it makes the rest of the employees feel the need to be more formal with me. "I don't care either way."

She makes a non-committal hum and looks out the window. "Do you need me to do anything while we travel?" she finally asks.

"Yes, I'll need to polish my presentation while we're in the air."

Her eyes dart over to mine nervously as she traps her lower lip between her teeth. My eyes pause there as my mind wanders down a path that would for sure lead to a sexual harassment settlement. But, fuck, does she have to do that especially with the vulnerability swirling around her? The more I study her, the more noticeable it becomes.

Her body language is all off. The way she's shrunk into herself. Even her clipped answers are devoid of her usual sunny personality.

"Clara." I infuse my voice with authority, forcing her to look at me. "Are you okay?"

An internal battle plays out behind her eyes before she breaks with a deep sigh. "No. I'm really nervous. I've never flown before."

"Oh," I say dumbly. I wasn't expecting that answer. "It's perfectly safe. Our pilots are current on all their licenses and requirements."

I can tell that hasn't done anything to ease her worries. I shuffle through the statistics I know off hand about flight travel safety, but I'm afraid nothing is truly comforting. As her attention moves back to the window, I pull up Google on my phone and start looking for comforting facts.

"According to the NTSB, the odds of surviving a plane crash are ninety-five percent." That's actually pretty surprising. "You are nineteen times safer in a plane than driving a car."

"I don't know how to drive," she mumbles.

I do a double take. "Really?"

"Yep, really."

"Where are you from, Clara?"

"I grew up in Oklahoma."

"How did you end up in Chicago?"

"Came here for college and never left."

That's odd. Her resume said nothing about her attending college.

"Where did you go to school?" I ask, genuinely curious.

"Northwestern," she answers quietly.

What the fuck?

"You went to Northwestern?" Why wouldn't she include that on her resume? "What was your degree in?"

"Business," she replies.

I mull this new information over. Why is someone with a degree in business from Northwestern working as a temp? Why doesn't she list her education on her resume? What else is she hiding?

I study her as she keeps her eyes focused out the window. I get the very clear feeling that she doesn't want to talk about herself. As the mystery surrounding Clara Snow deepens, I find myself more and more drawn to her.

I'm just about to ask some more probing questions when Tom pulls through the airport gate, driving right up to the hanger. I watch her eyes widen as we park beside the freshly painted Gulfstream. It was a bit of an extravagant purchase, but, at the end of the day, I need to be able to jump on a plane at a moment's notice, especially while I'm seeking investors to go global.

Tom opens the door beside me, and I grab my briefcase before stepping out. I offer my hand to Clara, unsure if she'll take it or not. A jolt of electricity runs through my veins as she slides her clammy palm against mine while she steps out of the town car.

She really is nervous. Maybe I should offer to let her stay behind. But when she doesn't immediately pull her hand away from mine, I find it hard to let go. She's staying with me today. Reluctantly, I release her hand and guide her toward the stairs.

"Good morning, Mr. Bennett." Mark, one of our pilots is waiting at the bottom of the steps with our head flight attendant, Catherine. "Flight path looks smooth and uneventful," he says.

"Great to hear." I place my hand on Clara's back. "This is Clara Snow, my temporary EA."

They greet each other, and Catherine nods demurely. I gesture for Clara to go up the metal steps first, trying to avoid noticing the way her hips sway as she walks up in her high heels. At least that trench coat she's wearing covers everything. I wonder if I can convince her keep it on all day.

Less than thirty seconds on the plane, and that thought is answered as Catherine takes Clara's coat. I have to focus on unbuttoning my suit jacket and draping it over a chair to force myself not to stare at Clara. Under that trench coat she's wearing a gray sweater dress. The neckline is high and modest but does nothing to hide the fact that Clara has a body with ridiculous curves. The dress hugs her chest down to her waist and then flares over her round hips and delectable ass.

Once again, my mind is wandering into pervy territory as I wonder what's underneath that dress. Somehow, I imagine her bras and panties are as chaotic as she can be. They probably never match or are themed somehow. Little

Christmas trees and Santa Claus faces dotting white cotton. A surge of desire makes my cock twitch.

What is wrong with me?

"Where should I sit?" she asks, looking lost in the middle of the cream-colored cabin.

"Right here." I point to the table I'll be working at. "We can sit side by side for take-off, and then I'll switch to the other side of the table."

"I'm sorry," she says before going back to chewing her lip.

"It's okay." Before my brain catches up with my hand, I cup her jaw and run my thumb under her lower lip. Her cheeks turn pink as heat races through my body. "You're chewing off your lipstick."

CHAPTER 7

CLARA

HIS VOICE IS husky as his thumb caresses my chin. The air between us thickens as his emerald eyes darken, zeroing in on my mouth. I release my lip, completely entranced by this strangely comfortable encounter.

"I have more lipstick in my purse. I can fix it before the meeting," I say quietly.

Hearing my voice seems to break him from whatever trance he was in. He snatches his hand back like touching me burned his skin. Maybe it did, it definitely made me feel something.

He motions for me to take the seat beside the window. I squeeze past him to sit, my ass brushes against him because, apparently, he has forgotten how to give a person space to maneuver. Our weird moment earlier has my mind all sorts of fucked up because now all I can focus on is how good he smells. I keep dragging greedy breaths through my nose trying to satiate my obsession with his scent.

"You're breathing weird," he says without looking at me.

"Your cologne is strong." I clear my throat. "It's a bit overpowering."

I am unprepared for the smirk he shoots me at that. "It's a custom fragrance from a perfumer in Paris. It was crafted to be powerful and memorable."

Jesus.

He got his money's worth then.

"Is it?" he asks.

"Is it what?"

"Powerful." He leans closer and lowers his voice. "Memorable."

Is he flirting?

"No, I completely forget about you as soon as I step out of the office."

His smile widens, flashing his perfectly straight, white teeth, and oh my fuck, he has a dimple. God clearly plays favorites. Also, who knew he had a sense of humor hidden up there beside the stick up his ass?

"I'll have to work on it."

"Please do. You could start with not being such a Scrooge about the Christmas decor."

A retort is just about to pass his lips when Catherine steps out of the galley. Her uniform is understated and classy, a navy pencil skirt and cream turtleneck with Tech-Jet's logo on it. She demurely smiles at both of us.

"What can I get you once we're in the air?" she asks.

"Coffee." Asher is back to his stoic persona.

"I'd like coffee, but this is my first time flying, so maybe a ginger ale if you have it?"

"Of course," she says as she taps her french manicured fingertips on the table. "Once the captain gives me the okay, I'll grab those for you."

As soon as the door closes behind her, I sense Asher relax beside me. Before I can question the change in the demeanor more, he speaks.

"If you get nervous, let me know. I can talk you through what's happening."

"Thank you," I say, genuinely grateful for his care. "I guess you probably fly around in your jet a lot, huh?"

"I do." He reaches around me, his arm crossing my body as he grabs the seat belt beside my hip. He's so close I can see the smallest flecks of gold around his pupil. I find myself holding my breath as he pauses in front of me, just the slightest hesitation before straightening back into his chair and buckling up himself.

I release my breath and remind myself that I'm sitting next to my boss. My wealthy, handsome, way out of my league, boss. I'm just imagining this tension, and if I don't stop, I'm going to make things incredibly awkward.

"I hope you enact policies at work and home to counter your carbon footprint."

He turns and gives me the side eye. "I've never given my carbon footprint a thought."

I scoff. Of course, he hasn't. He won't be one of the

people stuck on earth as it deteriorates. He'll be up in space with a galactic penthouse and alien servants.

"What are you grunting about?" His voice pulls me out of my thoughts.

"Nothing." I'm not about to tell him I just imagined a blue skinned alien in a French maid's uniform. "I just think that maybe you should explore ways to make sure your habits don't cause more harm than necessary."

"You do realize that my app is intended to make luxury travel easier, right? This," he gestures around the cabin, "is literally the lowest rung for the bar."

"I'll brainstorm some things for you to enact around the office."

He chuckles. "Or I could just write a check."

"There are more important things than money. Other, better, ways to have an impact."

"Not in my world."

I grip the arms of my chair as the plane jerks. My eyes immediately move to the window as we begin moving out of the building it was parked in. It can't be a good sign for me if my heart rate is already increasing before we're even in the air.

"Easy." Asher's voice has taken an uncharacteristically soft tone. "Just backing out of the hanger. Maybe you need something stronger than a ginger ale," he teases.

"Like a Xanax with a vodka chaser," I say under my breath.

A chuckle rumbles from his chest as I turn my attention to the window. The sky is lightening as the sun rises to our east. There are no clouds in the sky so that must be good. At least I hope so. I relax back into my seat as the plane moves forward slowly toward the runway.

"This isn't too bad," I say as the plane pauses.

Instantaneous regret fills me as the plane roars to life, speeding down the runway. I must cry out because I feel Asher's strong hand encompass mine as he links our fingers together, and I try to keep myself from falling apart.

The ground falls away below us, and my stomach flips at the sensation. That was both the most exhilarating and terrifying experience of my life. I close my eyes for a minute as my body settles down, and that's when I realize I'm still holding his hand. Not only that, but when I look down, I see his thumb sweeping across my knuckles lightly.

My stomach flips for a completely different reason. I know he's just being kind, but the reassuring gesture of comfort has my body awakening. When I move to pull my hand away, he tightens his grip, ever so slightly. His eyes search mine like he's struggling to uncover all my secrets through the contact of our palms.

"Sorry." I break the tension as I pull my hand from his.

"No apologies. I took your hand." He stands abruptly and moves to the other side of the table, just as he said he would. The soft look is gone from his eyes as he opens his laptop. "We need to go through my presentation. I can't risk fucking this up. This is the biggest private equity firm in the country."

One two-hour flight in Asher's jet and a much shorter but far more fraught with anxiety helicopter ride into the city, and we're sitting in a conference room full of grim faces. Most of those joining us are older men, but there are two women at the table. I feel substantially underdressed as the only one not in a suit, but I don't own one.

Asher spent every minute of our flight having me fire questions off at him and tweaking his presentation as soon as the plane leveled out. With each mile we traveled, I could feel him closing off and buttoning up. It's better that way. When he lets his guard down, I feel like I can trust him. Like I can open up and let him in.

I rarely feel that way with anyone. The closest I come is when I'm volunteering at the shelter. That's because those people understand my existence more than anyone else ever could, especially my boss, who was born with a silver spoon.

He pulls a chair out for me before taking the one to my left. I can't help but notice the way he flips a pen through his fingers. To most it probably looks like an absent-minded habit, but he's not the type to fidget. A younger man, one he seems to be familiar with, watches him closely.

"Can I take that pen from you?" I ask, leaning closely to whisper in his ear.

The movement immediately stops, and he hands it to me wordlessly.

The man across from us watches with curiosity. He had just been measuring up Asher, but now his gaze is locked on me. His eyes are a dark brown, nearly black, and give me an uneasy feeling. Revulsion slithers down my back as his eyes move down from my face to my chest.

"How am I just now realizing how stunning your new secretary is, Ash?" he says lecherously.

"She's my executive assistant, not secretary." Asher's voice is calm but laced with ice. "Sara is out on maternity leave through the new year."

Sleazy McDouchebag holds his hand toward me. "I'm Courtland Marshall. Ash and I go way back to college."

"Clara." I take his hand to shake, but he tips it down and kisses my knuckles instead. I pull my hand back quickly as a low grumble vibrates from Asher's chest.

Luckily the door closes, and an older man hobbles to the front of the room. He speaks for a few minutes and then gives Asher the floor. He stands, striding to the white board hanging on the wall and scrawling out line after line of numbers as he begins to speak about taking the company global.

He commands the room like always. No sign of nerves or uncertainty are ever visible. I should ask him for pointers before I go to the city zoning committee and ask them to allow the shelter to purchase the rest of the block.

By the time he finishes the presentation and fields questions, the entire room is eating out of his hand. I can practically see the dollar signs flickering in their eager eyes. As I stand and start putting everything Asher brought away, I feel a clammy hand land on the side of my waist.

"I'd love to show you around the city sometime. Have

you ever been to New York?" Courtland asks, his garlic breath puffing against my face as I look away.

"No, I haven't actually. But Asher flew us from the airport to the city in a helicopter. I got a pretty great view from there." I shift my weight and take a step back. His proximity has me incredibly uncomfortable.

"Oh, it's much better from below. Give me your number, and I'll fly you out sometime." His fingers dig into my back, refusing to let me go.

I take another step backwards, and my back connects with a wall of muscle shrouded in the most delicious, expensive smelling cologne. Asher guides me beside him, placing himself between Courtland and me. They bare their teeth at one another in what I assume should be smiles, but really it looks more like a declaration of war.

"Hands off my employee." Asher blocks me fully now.

"I was just trying to entice her out to see the city with me. You know there's no place like Manhattan at Christmas time."

"Chicago is pretty spectacular." He picks up his briefcase and stands to his full height, several inches over his foe. "Plus, Miss Snow is spoken for." He turns back to me. "Let's go. We've got a flight to catch back home."

"Here," Courtland says as he stops me. He slides his business card into my hand with a smarmy smile. "Give me a call when you're done working for Bennett."

"Clara." Asher glowers from the doorway.

"Nice meeting you," I say as I walk out to join my visibly irritated boss at the elevator bank.

The elevator doors open, and Asher motions me forward. He steps in behind me and jabs the button with more aggression than necessary. Waves of 'don't fuck with me' vibes roll off him as he stews beside me. I watch in awe as his jaw clenches so hard I'm surprised I can't hear his teeth cracking.

"Can I see that?" he points at the business card I'm still holding, his voice gritty.

"Sure."

He takes it from my outstretched hand and tears it in two and then tears it a second time. The elevator opens and he strides off in front of me, dropping the torn pieces into a trash can. My jaw drops as I watch him walk through the doors of the lobby and out onto the busy sidewalk. I scurry to catch up, wrapping my arm around his bicep and halting his momentum.

"What was that?" I stare up at him, annoyed by how he looks extra delicious in his pissy mood. "What if I wanted his contact information?" I didn't, but it doesn't change the fact that I might have.

"You don't." He shakes me off and heads toward the town car waiting for us. "I ordered a car back to the airport, so you don't have to deal with the discomfort of the helicopter."

Regardless of how kind that is, I'm not letting him get away with his awful behavior. "It takes a lot of audacity to decide who your temporary assistant does and does not want to form any type of relationship with."

"He's an asshole."

"So are you," I blurt before thinking.

He stares at me in what appears to be shock before his lips twitch, a smirk threatening. He opens the car door for me and gestures for me to get in. He slides in beside me, pressing his leg against mine from hip to ankle.

"I am, which is why you should listen to me. You shine too bright for some asshole to come along and dull your sparkle."

We're both quiet as his words sink in. "Thank you," I say quietly. "I'm sorry for calling you an asshole, that was incredibly out of line."

"True, though," he shrugs. He pulls his phone out and starts going through emails and messages.

"Can I help you with anything?"

"No, just relax for a bit. I need to handle these."

I sit back and turn my attention to the streets and buildings surrounding us. It's not that different from Chicago, but somehow it feels grittier. There are more people, and the energy is frenetic. I can't help but wonder where everyone is going. Some big penthouse in a skyscraper overlooking Central Park? A date at a trendy restaurant? A Broadway show? The possibilities are seemingly endless.

"How do you think it went?" Asher asks, pulling me from my reverie.

"I think it went great. Couldn't have been better."

"You think? I messed up with my presentation three times."

"I didn't notice." I turn toward him. "That says a lot

when I helped you work through everything on the flight here."

He makes a non-committal sound and glances out the window. The air around him thickens with doubt. His jaw muscle ticks again, and I have the craziest urge to smooth it out with my thumb. Instead, I open my mouth with the first thought to fly through my brain.

"I bet you hear from them with enough funding to get started on the next phase of expansion within twenty-four hours."

He gives me a dubious glance. "What are we betting?"

"Um..." I didn't know he'd even entertain the conversation. "I'll take my Christmas decorations down if I'm wrong."

His eyes light up with that term of the bet.

"But if I'm right, you have to come help me serve Thanksgiving dinner at the homeless shelter I volunteer at." He starts to open his mouth, but I silence him with my palm. "No, you can't just make a monetary donation. Action over checks."

His lips slam shut as he studies me. I know he hates my decorations, and he really seems to think he bombed this. I know otherwise, plus I'm sure I could find a work around to keep most of my decor.

He holds his hand out. "You have a deal, Miss Snow."

CHAPTER 8

ASHER

AFTER ANOTHER LONG night of thinking way too much about Clara and not enough about my business, I'm dragging ass on the way into work. I watched her disappear into her building and then saw the light flicker on in an apartment upstairs. Her neighborhood isn't the worst I've seen, but it's not the best either. I can't believe she lives there alone and commutes so often early in the morning and late at night.

As my employee, her safety is my priority, so I sent a car service to pick her up today as well as for the rest of her time working for me. It makes sense to do it this way anyway. She's out running errands for me all day; it'll make her more productive by easing her workload.

Nico strolls into my office and collapses into one of the

chairs across from me after setting a cup of coffee on my desk. "How did yesterday go?"

"I fucked up numbers three times. Fucking Courtland Marshall was there."

He winces, knowing the history between us. "That guy is a piece of shit. Always has been, always will be."

"He kept flirting with Clara."

"And," he asks with raised eyebrows, "is that a problem?"

"Yes," I answer too forcefully. I adjust my tie and lower my voice. "She's too nice for someone like him."

"Ash," Nico says after a long beat of silence. "Do you have a thing for Clara?" I can't help but notice the way hope colors his tone.

"No." I meet his eyes straight on. "Absolutely not. She's my employee. She's too nice and sunshine-y. I mean, look at her desk." I gesture through the clear glass wall. "It looks like the North Pole exploded out there." She now has a tiny train set and holiday village winding around the table-top tree she started her décor with.

"She is nice and," he pauses, trying to find the right word, "festive."

I nod, glad he's not going to push some romantic agenda on me.

"But she's also fucking smart. I talked to her the other day for almost forty minutes about torts, and she never looked lost or bored."

"Yeah, she went to Northwestern for an MBA and a degree from the center for law studies." Both of which she neglected to inform me of yesterday when she told me she graduated from there.

"Why the fuck is she working as a temp, then?" he asks as his brows furrow.

"Your guess is as good as mine." I scratch my jaw as movement from the elevators pulls my attention. "I might put Stella on it. See if she can figure it out."

Clara steps off the elevator with her lips pressed together in a thin line and eyes narrowed in my direction. She stops at her desk to drop her purse in the drawer and hang her coat up but then comes straight for me.

"May I have a moment, Mr. Bennett?" She asks with a venom-laced tone.

"I was just leaving," Nico stands and nods as he passes her. "Good morning, Clara."

"Good morning Mr. James," she replies warmly before turning her icy glare on me.

Nico looks at me over her head and mouths "You fucked up," before closing the door behind him. I hit the button on my desk that turns the glass opaque and turn my attention to her. She should look ridiculous in the dress she's wearing today. It's a deep green velvet with white trim, she looks like an escaped elf. If elves at the North Pole moonlighted as Marilyn Monroe performers on their days off. Seriously, the curves on this woman's body are mouthwatering.

"Why did you send a car service for me this morning?"

"For efficiency." I lean back in my chair as she stands across from me, fuming. "I didn't realize how far out you lived. Now you won't have to rely on public transportation."

"I don't mind taking the L."

"I prefer my assistants arrive and leave in a timely manner."

"I've never been late," she cries out. "It is an egregious overstep to send a car for me."

"It's not. It makes more sense from a business standpoint."

"Really?" she crosses her arms over her chest. "Do you send cars for all your employees? Or is it just because of the neighborhood I live in? Is it not good enough for you? Too dangerous? Because trust me, I've lived in way worse situations surrounded by people who are ten times worse than anyone on my block."

I stand and lean against my hands on my desk. "There are bars across the windows on your building."

She mirrors my stance, leaning across the desk back toward me. "I might be young, but trust me when I tell you that I can handle myself and my safety."

Fuck.

I want to grab her by the ponytail and drag her across my desk. My dick is hardening by the second as I look down into her stormy gray eyes spitting ice at me. I know she's capable, but fuck if I don't want to protect her anyway.

Her lips are parted as she looks up at me, the silence crackling with sexual tension mixed with anger. How have I never noticed the beauty mark on her left cheekbone? Before I think better of it, I lift my hand to her cheek and run my thumb over the spot. She leans into my touch for the briefest moment before backing away.

"I appreciate the concern, but I don't need a car service." Her voice is softer but raspy, giving me just enough room to push back.

"Tough," I say as my hand falls back to my side, already missing the warmth of her smooth skin beneath it. "It's been arranged."

The door swings open and Stella waltzes in. Thank fuck, because I'm not sure I would have survived going any more rounds with Clara without stripping her down and seeing what she's wearing under that ridiculous dress. Stella looks back and forth between us with a keen eye, probably trying to figure out what was happening in here.

"Am I interrupting?" she asks.

"No, we were just clearing up some job expectations for Miss Snow."

Clara's eyes narrow on me but she nods. "I'll order your breakfast, Mr. Bennett." The sass she throws into my name makes my cock twitch.

Stella stares me down with wide eyes until the door clicks shut behind Clara. She arches one of her brows with a knowing look. "You want her."

I start to deny it, but if there was anyone this knowledge was safe with, it'd be Stella. Plus, she'd call me on my bullshit anyway. So, I drop to my chair with a defeated and pained nod. "I shouldn't want her, but I do."

"Don't be such a fucking drama queen." She sits and crosses her legs. "It's not the worst thing in the world. And for what it's worth, I love her. She has such good vibes."

"She does, doesn't she?" Her whole spirit feels so pure,

not in an innocent type of way but just her outlook on life. "She called me out on the way to New York for my carbon footprint, and when I asked for a recommendation of a charity to donate to as way to offset it, she called me out again. A whole lecture on how you can't throw money at problems."

Stella tosses her head back and laughs. "Pure gold."

"Then she made a bet with me that I'd get the funding for the next step, and if she wins the bet I have to volunteer at a homeless shelter on Thanksgiving."

She stops laughing and grins from ear to ear. "Oh, I really love her now." She takes a dramatic pause. "Because you got the funding."

CHAPTER 9

CLARA

I'M STILL STEWING in annoyance at Asher's blatant and, honestly, offensive violation of appropriate boundaries. I love my neighborhood and rarely feel unsafe. Just because I don't live in a high rise off Wacker doesn't mean I need a driver. I mean, fuck, I work in corporate America as a young woman, that's probably statistically just as dangerous.

Taking the L allows me time to read my cozy mysteries or catch up on the news. Sometimes I'll just people watch, making up theories about what people do or where they live. Half the time people are going to or from the airport on the line I take, so there's many things to theorize.

My phone vibrates with a notification that Asher's breakfast is nearby, so I head down to the lobby to meet the delivery driver. Taylor joins me waiting for the elevator. As we make small talk, I feel the weight of Asher's gaze on my back. The elevator door opens, and Taylor places his hand on my back, guiding me on first. It feels nothing beyond a friendly touch, but when I turn my head as I step on, my eyes meet Asher's cold stare.

Taylor keeps talking, but I'm not listening. I can't help but wonder what that look was for. Surely, he can't be angry with me for refusing his ridiculous offer. He didn't really look mad though, it was a different emotion swirling in those green depths.

"What do you say?" Taylor asks as we step out into the lobby.

"Hmm?" I ask, surprised by the question.

"You didn't hear a word I said, did you?" he asks with a light-hearted smile. "I asked if you want to go grab drinks after work today. I'm meeting a few friends."

"Oh, yes. I'd love to. Thanks for asking."

"Awesome," he gives me a smile and walks back toward the kitchen while I go meet the driver outside.

Asher is sitting behind his desk on a call when I get back up to my desk. I watch to gauge whether I should enter or not. He looks exasperated as he runs his hand through his dark hair. He looks up and sees me, motioning me inside. I set the bag on his desk, and he motions for me to sit in the chair as he listens to whoever is on the other line.

"Mom, I have to let you go but don't worry about the gala. I have everything under control." A faint smile plays upon his lips as he listens for another few seconds. "Yes, I'll see you Saturday for brunch. Bye."

He ends the call and sets the phone on his desk before looking at me. "Parents," he says in the way most would relate to.

My mood darkens just a bit. It's not his fault, it's not my fault that I can't relate, but sometimes it feels like getting sucker punched. There are still moments in my life where I would give just about anything to know what it feels like to have another human on this planet care enough to nag me.

"Good news," he says as he digs into the bag for his breakfast. He looks up as he pulls out the omelet, his hand stopping halfway to the desk. "What's wrong?" he asks abruptly.

"What?" I ask surprised. "Nothing."

"Not nothing. You look sad," he answers.

"Nope. Just still annoyed," I latch onto the most logical reason for the change. Truthfully, I'm completely taken aback that he picked up on the shift of my mood so easily and clearly.

His eyes narrow as he looks at me. I don't think he believes me, but he doesn't push either. "You won the bet."

It takes a minute for the news to sink in, but when it does, I launch from my chair with a cheer. "I told you." I clasp my hands in front of me. "Congratulations. Well-earned and deserved, Mr. Bennett."

"Thank you." He nods and looks up at me with the softest smile I've seen on his handsome face. "But please call me Asher from now on."

"I'll do my best." I sit back down. "I'm holding you to our bet."

"I wouldn't dream of backing out."

"Should we invite Stella and Nico? I bet Taylor would come, too." My mind is already racing about ways to pull more people in.

"No," he says abruptly. "Just us is fine."

"Oh," I say, the wind knocked from my sails. "We should do something to celebrate for the company though." I tap a finger against my lip as I think. "A catered meal is boring, and I'm assuming you have a holiday party already planned, so that's out."

"We don't do holiday parties," he answers.

"What?" I ask incredulously. "How do you employ this many people and not have a holiday party?"

"I don't celebrate them myself beyond a dinner with my family. It's just never occurred to me."

"I'll organize one." I make it a statement, not a question, because nothing is stopping me. Not even Mr. Scrooge sitting across from me. "It'll be difficult on short notice, but I can make it happen."

His eyes move back and forth between mine as he sits there like a king on a throne, his breakfast is probably cold in front of him. "It would make you happy to do that, wouldn't it?"

I'm not sure why my happiness figures into his decision making, but I answer him anyway. "Absolutely. Give me a budget, and I'll make it happen."

"I'm probably going to regret this but talk to Stella. You two come up with a plan and a budget." He holds a hand up as I start to thank him. "But I need something from you in return."

"Anything." I'm so excited I'd probably give him the shirt off my back if he asked.

"You'll be my plus one for a charity gala my family is involved with. Do you have a passport?"

"I—" shock has stolen my ability to speak. "I do, actually." I went to a conference in Toronto in college. "But I don't have a dress." I doubt I could pull together enough money for one at this point anyway. And why do I need a passport?

"Don't worry about the dress. Stella can take you to find one. You can take a whole day to plan the party and find a dress."

"Where is the gala?"

"Paris. It'll be a working weekend. I have a few meetings set up already."

Paris.

A city I never imagined visiting in my wildest dreams. I'm already creating a list of places I'd love to see, even if we just drive past them. Ranking must see, if possible, places.

"Do we have a deal?" he asks as he stands, holding his hand out across the desk.

"Deal." A spark runs up my arm as my palm meets his.

"I don't think this is the type of place we should be shopping at for me," I tell Stella as we pull up in front of a boutique on Michigan Avenue. "I'm more of an outlet mall kind of girl."

Two guards stand just inside the entrance of the boutique, both give me a dubious once over until Stella takes my arm and nods at each. The light from the crystal chandeliers reflects off the marble floors as a salesperson approaches us, champagne in hand.

"Ms. James, welcome back," the red-haired woman says. "Should we start pulling for you?"

"No." Stella gestures at me. "Francesca, this is Clara Snow. She needs a few pieces for a business function and charity gala in Paris this weekend."

"How wonderful," her brown eyes turn to me giving me a thorough once over. "Ashley let's start pulling some dresses for Ms. Snow. Black tie, I presume?"

"Yes," Stella breaks away from me and wanders off with Francesca and Ashley.

I hear them murmuring as I walk through the racks. This is not a place I would ever choose myself. The clothes have no price tags, and there's only a few small sizes out on the floor. I know for a fact my size twelve body won't be squeezing into these size two and four couture dresses.

The guards keep a discrete eye on me as I make my way over to the jewelry display. A pair of teardrop emerald and diamond earrings catch my eye. They are absolutely stunning, and one of the only things I would ever splurge on, not that I could afford them in a thousand lifetimes.

I pull myself away from the jewelry and move onto the shoes. Stilettos line the shelves from nude to black in all styles. Interspersed among the shoes are other accessories like posh hats you'd see on a British monarch and silk scarves with the fashion house's emblem printed on them.

"Clara," Stella calls, "we have a few options pulled."

"I'm surprised you found options for me. Everything on the floor seemed to be in limited sizes," I say to her as I walk back into a curtained changing room and Stella drops to the velvet settee in front of the three-way mirror.

"We have an in-house tailor for any adjustments you might need." Francesca steps inside the room with me, placing one more dress on the hook. "I know there are quite a few but humor me with this green one. I think it'll look stunning with your coloring."

She disappears back behind the curtain before I can reply. That's when I realize how right she was. Dresses in various jewel tones and black hang from every available inch of the wall. I run my fingers over the material of each, automatically dismissing two dresses based on feel alone.

I pick out one of the black dresses, a long gown with a high neckline and high slit. I undress and step into the gown and zip the dress as high as I can reach. Stella looks up as soon as I step out and stands to come finish zipping me up.

"This looks incredible." She looks over my shoulder as I stand in front of the mirror.

I lift my arms to look at the sides and see way too much side boob. "Immediately no."

"What? Side boob is hot. A little tape and they'll be lifted and perky."

"I haven't had perky boobs since I was twelve," I say

with a laugh. "Plus, I'm going with my boss who definitely isn't interested in seeing my boobs."

Stella's eyes meet mine in the mirror as she suppresses a comment. "Let me grab the zipper."

The next few dresses all go the same way, they look good, but the slit is too high, or the material falls weird over my stomach. Finally, the only dress left is a deep green, long-sleeved, backless dress. When I step out of the dressing room, I know this is one by the look on everyone's face. I step onto the dais in front of the mirror and look at myself in all the angles.

"It is stunning." Stella walks around me and lifts my hair into a messy bun. "Definitely the one. You'll need to wear your hair up. Maybe a pair of statement earrings."

"I don't have anything that would do this dress justice." I don't even know if I can afford this dress, I have some savings I can dip into if necessary. "How much is it?" I ask Francesca.

"Don't worry about it," Stella says before she can answer. "Ash is covering everything for the gala."

"What?" I screech. "No, he is not."

"Ladies," Francesca says stepping between us. "I brought this pair of earrings out just to get an idea of what type of earring to look for to accessorize." She hands me the earrings I was drooling over earlier.

I don't even know if I want to touch them, let alone put them inside my earlobe. My desire to see them on wins, though, as I begin putting them in. "Just out of curiosity, how much are these?"

"Seventy-eight," Francesca answers as she looks over the dress.

"Seventy-eight hundred?" I clarify. That would make these earrings the most expensive thing I've ever touched.

"Seventy-eight thousand, dear."

A distressed gasp comes from my throat as I hastily, but very fucking carefully, remove them and hand them back to her. I'm in so far over my head here. What the hell am I even doing? How did I get to this place in my life?

I glance over my shoulder to the door, very seriously contemplating making a run for it. Maybe it is time for a new city to explore and settle into for a few years. I always said I wouldn't stay in one place. I've gotten too comfortable in Chicago.

"Calm down," Stella hands me a glass of champagne. "You look like you are about to have a breakdown."

"I am."

The tailor comes to take a few measurements to make sure the chain that runs across the back to keep the sides held together is the correct length, and we go back and forth on the height of the slit in the front of my dress.

By the end of the day, I have a dress and shoes, courtesy of Asher, and several new skirts and sweaters for the two days we're going to be working, courtesy of my emergency savings account. But if a once in a lifetime trip to Paris, even if it is a work trip, isn't reason enough to use some of the money I've saved over the years, I don't know what is.

CHAPTER 10

ASHER

"YOU KNOW with all the money you have, you could pay someone to pack for you," Nico says from where he's sprawled on my bed watching me pack for Paris.

"Where would the fun be in that?" I ask drolly.

I honestly haven't been able to get the photo that Stella took of Clara out of my mind. The deep, rich green of that dress against her creamy complexion immediately did me in. I could only see her from the side, but that didn't stop me from staring at my phone for an hour and thirteen minutes yesterday afternoon.

When I went to pick up my tuxedo today, I stopped by the boutique picked up her dress and everything else I purchased for her. It's a bit more than she thought I was doing, and I'm probably pushing my luck. To be honest I don't give a fuck. I'm going to gift her whatever I want, and she can deal with it.

"Where are you staying while you're there?"

"My penthouse."

I went to a boarding school in the northeast for all my secondary education, which is where I met Stella and Nico, but I spent my summers in an international business school in Paris. The penthouse with a view overlooking the Eiffel Tower was the first large purchase I made when I came into my inheritance at twenty-one.

It was a hasty decision, and one I probably should have thought harder about, but I renovated the space and now my family and friends use it as needed. I don't even want to imagine how many orgies Nico has hosted within those walls. And while I often feel jaded about Paris, I know that the space is always warm and welcoming, even when the city is not.

"Nice. What hotel are you putting Clara up at?"

"I should book her a room at a hotel," I mumble. "I'm having her stay with me. It's not like there isn't room."

Nico sits up from his prone position and follows me into my closet like a needy puppy. "Back up. You've never had Sara stay in your private residences before."

I look over my shoulder at him and hit him with my boardroom glare. I should have known better than to try that on him because he hits me with his cross-exam raised eyebrow. The only one who could break this stalemate is Stella.

"Move," I say as I shoulder check him out of the way.

"No." He grabs my arm. "I'm going to give you advice."

"As my legal counsel or my friend?"

"Both." He releases me. "As your attorney, I'm going to advise you to tread carefully. A harassment lawsuit from a temp this close to going global could end you."

"Nothing I haven't thought of a million times already." I cross my arms and lean a hip against the mahogany dresser.

"But, as your friend, I think she could be great for you. An actual human to soften your edges instead of just warming your bed to scratch an itch."

"The contradictory advice is great," I reply sarcastically. "Very helpful."

"That's what I'm here for." He slaps my shoulders. "Speaking of advice, don't take that suit." He grabs the hanger in my hand and disappears back into my closet.

Two hours later, and I have two bags packed full of way too many options and a mind reeling with warring choices. A few times I even pull up the number for the hotel nearest my penthouse, but something stops me every time. Instead, I find myself pulling strings to make her first European trip memorable. We won't have much time to sightsee but the thought of watching her take in the lights on the Eiffel Tower or walking the halls of The Louvre pushes me to make accommodations in my schedule.

As I toss and turn in bed, I reach for my phone. I know I shouldn't pull up the photo Stella sent me, but I do it anyways. Apparently, my impulse control is shit when it comes to my beautiful, mysterious temp. I can't stop thinking about how smooth her skin looks. It's flawless.

She is flawless.

"Good morning," I say to a surprised Clara as she opens her door.

"What are you doing up here?" She's holding a black cat in one arm and a mascara wand in her other hand. "I still have," she checks the time on the tv, "eight minutes before I'm supposed to be downstairs."

"I think the more important question is whether you realize just anyone can waltz in your building. Shouldn't that door downstairs at least lock?"

"Did you waltz in?" She thrusts the cat at me and moves to a mirror over the sink in the kitchen, swiping mascara along her lashes. "I'm impressed you managed to get past Old Joe on the floor by the door with your happy feet."

"Is that what that lump of flesh was on the stairs?" I ask as I look around her apartment.

It's small. Smaller than my primary suite at home. But clean and organized, with plants hanging in every corner and the bed pushed against the wall with a window. The L goes racing by metal screeching on metal, and I swear to fuck the entire room shakes. Feels like it's one strong gust from toppling over.

"Don't judge my apartment." She points a finger at me. "I love this place."

"I'm not," I say with my hands slightly held up while still hanging onto the cat. "I'm just glad if you ever moved to

California, you'd be prepared for what a six-point magnitude earthquake feels like."

"Did your fancy schools come with a complementary theater degree, you ridiculous drama queen?"

"No, but I do have some carpentry skills if you want me to reinforce a few walls."

She fights a smile as she turns her attention to filling her cat food bowls. "I know your family owns a development and construction company, but I cannot imagine you in anything other than a fancy suit."

"Have you tried?" I set the cat down on the bed and cross the room toward her.

"Tried what?" she asks as she fills a water bowl, unaware of my approach.

"Imagining me in anything other than a suit?" I reach around her to grab the handle of her suitcase, caging her between myself and the counter.

She stills and turns slightly, those gorgeous gray eyes lock on mine as her lips part. Her gaze dips to my mouth before moving back up. Tension thickens the atmosphere of the tiny apartment.

This is a dangerous game. I should back off. But I can't pull myself away from her when I feel this pull. Especially knowing she feels it, too. I want to set her on this counter and bury my face in her pussy. I want to know how she sounds when she comes undone.

"I have," she admits softly in a sultry voice. "Sometimes, when you really piss me off, I imagine you dressed in a clown suit with a big red nose and shoes that squeak when you walk."

I laugh and shake my head. Had anyone else said that I would be pissed. She might have won this battle, but I'm going to win the war.

CHAPTER 11

CLARA

I KEPT my distance on the flight, only interacting with him when necessary for work. For a second inside my apartment, I thought he might kiss me. I would have let him. I would have let him do a lot of things.

My entire body lights up when he's near me, like he's a heat seeking missile, and I'm a beacon for destruction. And no doubt about it, he would cause total destruction in my life. I have to keep reminding myself that I'm just disposable to someone like him. Hell, I'm disposable to everyone in my life. I like it like that, it's my comfort zone.

How would I even exist in any other space beyond replaceable? Forgettable? My cat and the shelter are the only constants I need in my life.

The problem is, despite his grumpy, prickly personality,

I see the depth that's there. The way he wants me to be safe getting to and from work. The way he held my hand through takeoff and landing. His shell is asshole, but his inside is teddy bear. He makes me feel safe and seen, the most dangerous thing of all.

"We'll be landing shortly," Asher says as he takes the seat beside me. "A car will take us directly to my penthouse."

"Then on to my hotel, I presume?"

"You'll be staying with me. There's a large guest suite with a private sitting room and bathroom."

"I don't want to put you out," I begin to say.

"It's not an imposition," he interrupts me. "It just makes sense for us to stay together for maximum efficiency. I promise you'll have all the privacy you need."

"Makes sense."

"Tonight, we'll have dinner with a few investors at their home just outside the city."

"Do you spend a lot of time here? In Paris?"

"I spent my summers in secondary school here. My mom is American but grew up in Paris. She wanted us to have the cultural experience, and my dad wanted us to be business focused, so my brothers and I all did internship programs here."

I squeeze my eyes shut as the plane touches down, and my body is flung forward. Feeling the warmth of Asher's hand as it lands on my leg brings me a little peace at the still foreign sensation of going from the air to land. He leaves it there, his thumb occasionally brushing my knee, until we stop just outside a hanger.

My nose is pressed to the glass the entire drive to his penthouse. The first glimpse of the Eiffel Tower makes me squeal with excitement. Even against the gray, overcast sky it is magnificent. I look over at Asher, who's watching me with a small smile.

"Is it always so incredible?"

"I was a toddler the first time I saw it, so I didn't really care. To be honest, I still don't." He chuckles when my face falls. "I didn't mean to burst your bubble. It's beautiful at night with the light show."

"Well now I don't believe you," I tease, turning my attention back out the window. "It's so different from Chicago. So much older and worldlier. Almost like you can feel the history living and breathing around you."

"I guess if history smells like piss and cigarette smoke."

I turn back to him, completely scandalized, and smack his thigh as he laughs some more. "Stop that."

"Okay," he says with another chuckle. "I'll stop for real this time. After the gala tomorrow night, I'll have the driver take us by some sights."

"Really?"

"Of course. It's your first international trip, we have to at least drive by some places."

The car stops, and I follow him out onto the sidewalk. Wicker chairs and small tables sit out in front of a bistro on the corner. A few people sit, sipping coffee or smoking, bundled in warm outerwear. I look up at the building in front of us, taking in the older looking facade. I don't know why I'm surprised to see he bought a home in a historic-looking building, but I am. I would have figured he'd find something more modern and showier.

The surprises don't end as we enter his flat.

"I have the entire top floor of the building. It's not all open concept like we're used to back in the states. I'll walk you through everything."

He leads me through a small foyer with a beautiful arrangement of flowers on a marble topped table and into a large sitting room. The walls are white with floor-to-ceiling windows and light parquet floors. I can see wrought iron balconies off a set of french doors in the middle of the room. A bar is set up in the corner of the room as well as two seating areas with comfortable but luxurious looking furniture.

From there we move through a large dining room, a surprisingly modest kitchen, and into a library. All the walls are covered in rich, dark wood built-in shelves and cabinets. A desk sits in front of the doors leading out to another balcony. A quick scan of the titles tells me they're all in French.

We walk out into a corridor, and he points at the end of the hall.

"That's my room down there. That door leads to two rooms my brothers use when they come and a bathroom. Your suite of rooms is back down this way."

He leads me back to the foyer and into another large sitting area that mirrors the first we walked through. Then he leads us through a doorway into a large bedroom. The room is light and airy with long, gauzy window coverings and a large, pillowy, king-size bed in the middle. The bathroom is floor-to-ceiling marble, white with dainty gold veins. A crystal chandelier hangs in the middle, with a glass shower in one corner and a claw foot tub in the other.

"This is gorgeous." I look over at him. "The entire place is stunning."

"Thank you. This was the first property I ever bought on my own." He runs a hand over the marble wall. "It took a long time to align it to my vision, but now that we're here, it's worth it." He glances down at his watch. "We have a couple of hours to rest before dinner. I'll let you get settled in; your bags should be in the closet."

I watch as he walks out of the room, trying my damnedest not to watch the way his ass is perfectly hugged by the pants he's wearing. The scent of his cologne lingers in the air as I kick off my shoes and lie down on the bed. It's as heavenly as it looks. Before long I'm dozing off, barely remembering to set an alarm, so I'll have time to get ready.

"You look lovely," Asher says as he meets me in the foyer, his forest green eyes traveling up and down my body.

I chose a faux leather brown skirt and cream sweater paired with a pair of nude pumps. My hair falls around my shoulders in soft waves and, as usual, I kept my makeup minimal. Even with a three-inch boost, I still have to arch my neck to look up at him.

"As do you." He's the most casual I've seen him, in tweed trousers, a mocha-colored turtleneck sweater and a pair of sinfully sexy glasses. Thank fuck he doesn't wear those to the office. "I like the glasses."

"*Merci*," he says. "Traveling always dries out my eyes." He holds out my coat and helps me into it before putting his on.

"Is it going to be a problem that I don't know any French? I would have tried to learn but there wasn't time."

"No, it'll be fine. Tonight, is just a small gathering of people I've known for years. They all speak English."

"Okay, good. I just don't want to stick out too much as the obnoxious American," I say as I slide into the town car.

"Just don't smile too much."

"What?" I look over at him, stricken. I'm just a good ol' girl from Oklahoma. My smile is my armor.

He looks at me as though he's trying to dig for all my secrets before he responds. "Frequent smiles are a uniquely American trait. It's like walking around with a bald eagle on your shoulder in Europe. Easy tell."

"I think that's kind of depressing."

"It is what it is."

"You're very cynical, Mr. Bennett."

"Indeed, Miss Snow." He leans forward and gives instructions to the driver in French.

I could listen to that all day. I knew it was a romantic language but hearing Asher bark orders in it drenches my panties. If he keeps that up, I won't be able to kill the mood the next time he starts flirting with me.

Would it be so bad if something did happen between us? I think about that question all night as I watch him morph back into business mode. No smiles. No easy conversation. Everything is deal, everything is serious.

"He is very handsome, no?" his friend's wife, Nicolette, asks in thickly accented English.

"Asher?" I glance at her and then back to him. "He's my boss, but, yes, he is."

"He doesn't look at you like an employee."

"What?" I do a double take at her as she hands me another glass of champagne.

"He stares at you when you're not looking. His eyes always seek you out."

I laugh softly. "Probably because he's worried I'm going to mess up one of his deals."

"*Non*, he wants you. I know powerful men, and it is not concern on his face, it is hunger."

"What do you guys put in this champagne?" I joke as I peer down into my glass.

"What are you two talking about over here in the corner?" Asher asks as he joins us.

"How handsome you are," Nicolette replies.

Champagne shoots from my nose as I choke in surprise.

"*Je suis désolé,*" she hands me a napkin to wipe my face. The mischievous gleam in her eyes make me think she's not sorry at all.

"Is that so?" Asher asks smugly.

"In a conventional way." I can feel the heat of my surely

red cheeks. The earth could swallow me whole right now, and I'd die happy to never relive this moment.

He smirks at me, the first sign of humor I've seen all night, before turning his attention to Nicolette. "Good evening. We'll see you tomorrow."

He guides me out to the car with a hand on the small of my back. His palm lands on the car door as I pull on the handle, stopping my progress. I can feel the heat of his body as he leans into me.

"Conventional is boring. Mundane."

"It can be." I turn to face him, leaning a hip against the car. "Or it can be classic. Debonair."

"Which am I?"

"I think your ego's been fed enough tonight."

"Classic then," he says with a lopsided grin as he opens the door for me.

"You're insufferable."

"You'll be changing your tune in a few minutes."

"Why's that?"

"It's a surprise."

CHAPTER 12

ASHER

HER FACE FALLS as I tell her it's a surprise, and she looks out the window. Anxiety floods me as I try to figure out what just happened. We were bantering back and forth, and she was having a good time. Now, suddenly, she's withdrawn and sad.

"Hey." I reach over and squeeze her knee. "What just happened?"

"I don't like surprises." Her voice is dull and quiet, and nothing at all like the vivacious woman I've come to enjoy.

"Why?" I might be pressing my luck, but we have time.

I watch as she wars with herself on how much to divulge. Finally, she turns to me. "I was a foster child from the age of fourteen months on. There were times I'd go to school thinking I'd come home like a regular day, only to be pulled out in the middle of class. It messes with you, to never know when the next move was coming. Who's home you would land in. If it was safe." She gives me a sad smile. "I don't know if I'll ever learn to like surprises."

"I had no idea."

"I know." Her eyes turn glassy as she turns back toward the window. "How would you have known? I'm not much of an open book." Light reflects off a single tear as it rolls down her cheek.

"Clara." I say her name with a quiet demand. When she turns her face back to me, I reach up and wipe the tear from her face. "Thank you for trusting me with that part of you."

She rolls her lips in to stop them from trembling and takes a deep breath. "You're still insufferable."

I squeeze her thigh one last time and chuckle. "And you're a real piece of work. Pretty mouthy for an employee."

"I'm not the one who keeps taunting his employee," she sasses back. "Now, tell me the surprise."

I point out the window over her shoulder as we cross the Pont d'Iena. "Just look out your window."

"Oh my god," she screeches. "Oh my god!"

The look of excitement and joy on her face when she turns to me fills me with an odd warmth. Gone is the sad melancholy aura that not long ago lingered around her. It's been replaced with wonder and giddiness. I want to put that smile on her face again and again. Her eyes widen even more as the driver pulls over.

"Are we stopping?" She looks out of the car and back at me. "Can I get out?"

"No one is going to stop you."

She flings the door open before the driver can even get to her side. She's jumping with her arms in the air as I get out and share a look of amusement with the driver. Her exuberance is contagious, even to the most cynical of men. I pull out my phone to take a few pictures to send her, so she'll always have a reminder of this moment.

"*Monsieur, je pendrai des photos.*" He motions to my phone and then Clara.

"*Merci,*" I tell him as I hand my phone to him.

I walk over to Clara who is currently taking a video and excited bobbing up and down. I spin her around to face our driver. "He said he'd take a photo."

"Oh," she says as she slides out from under my arm, "I'll give him my phone, too."

"No need. I'll send them to you." I pull her back beside me, pleased as fuck when she presses against me.

"You're still insufferable, Bennett," she jokes.

I throw my head back with a laugh. "You're still a piece of work, Snow."

I take her phone and snap a few photos of her posing in ridiculous ways before suggesting we walk around a bit. Other tourists dot the area, but it's far from crowded. I really want to ask her more questions, but I don't know how to approach it or if they'd even be welcomed.

"Go ahead and ask," she says as we walk. "Everyone has questions, and I can feel them piling up inside that head of yours."

"I don't know much about the foster system. I don't want to ask something insensitive."

"The fact that you say that makes me believe you wouldn't be insensitive, but how does this sound, I'll give you bullet points? Answer all the frequently asked questions and you can add anything else on?"

"Sounds good." I'm relieved. I want to know everything but not at the cost of her comfort.

"My mom was an addict and a sex worker before she became pregnant with me. There's no father listed on my birth certificate, so I have to assume it was some random guy. She didn't realize she was pregnant until she was almost six months along but was clean from then until I was a year old. I was a high-needs baby with a few challenges but nothing long lasting from her drug use.

"She kept a steady minimum wage job until right after my first birthday when the factory she was working at closed suddenly. She went back to sex work and eventually drugs and overdosed."

"I'm sorry." I reach down and grab her hand, squeezing to give comfort.

"It's okay. I actually don't hold any ill will against her. I think she tried her hardest, but we lived in a shitty town with a lack of opportunities." She leaves her hand in mine but looks away. "Because I was labeled a high-needs child, no one showed interest in adopting me. As I aged up it became obvious I'd be a product of the foster system, and it was okay sometimes. Other times, it was not."

"Did you ever feel safe?" I blurt the question without

thinking. I just can't wrap my mind around growing up with such a different existence. The instability.

"Yeah." She gives me a sad smile. "There was one family in particular who were amazing. I lived with them for two years, and the first night I stayed with them they made this meal of kid-friendly food. It wasn't fancy, just frozen chicken nuggets, mixed berries, and crinkle fries. I colored with their kids and another foster child they had at the time until it was time to eat. Then the mom ran me a bath and brushed the tangles out of my hair, which no one had brushed my hair for me in years at that point."

She turns to me, and I tuck a piece of windblown hair behind her ear. I want so badly to kiss her, to wrap my arms around her and shield her from anything else horrible the world could throw at her. Instead, she takes a step back, and I let her.

"Thank you."

"For what?"

"For asking and not judging. For reminding me of such a beautiful memory." She turns and tilts her head back. "And for bringing me here. One thing to check off my bucket list."

I'm tempted to ask for that list, the desire to tick every box and add a million more riding me hard. But it's getting cold, and I know we need to get back.

CHAPTER 13

CLARA

AFTER DIVULGING my life story to Asher last night, I tossed and turned for hours. Despite how uncomfortable it is to be openly vulnerable like that, once I started, I couldn't stop. He seemed genuinely interested in the moment, but what does he think now that I've spilled the truth? Will the morning light shine a bit differently on me in his mind?

I'm already up by the time my alarm goes off and in need of coffee, so I find my way to the kitchen. I breathe a sigh of relief at the sight of a single cup system and not some fancy French coffee setup. I select a pod of hazelnut-flavored coffee and slide it in the slot.

While I wait for it to brew, I walk over to the window and take in the view of the buildings in the pink light of dawn. It feels otherworldly compared to what I'm used to seeing in Chicago. Even the old parts of the city are new in comparison to this.

"Good morning," Asher says, startling me.

"You scared me." I press a hand to my chest. "Good morning."

"Sorry," he says with a mischievous grin.

Now that I've turned around, I'm nearly speechless. Standing before me shirtless in a pair of low-slung gray sweatpants and those incredibly attractive glasses, I have to remind myself that he's my boss. My grumpy, arrogant boss, who pisses me off left and right. I knew he was fit from the way I could sometimes see his muscle through his shirt, but I wasn't expecting to see the planes of muscle across his chest and shoulders down to his abs and that sexy as sin Adonis belt pointing right at his cock.

Don't look at his cock, Clara.

I'm looking at his cock outline. The intrusive thoughts won't stop. Why is it so big? Must be a show-er and not a grower. A third leg. A tripod.

Stop it.

"I didn't realize you'd be up so early."

He stands beside me and reaches for a pod as if he has no idea how he's affecting me. How could he not know? I'm pretty sure I feel drool on my chin. I haven't had sex in so long I'm pretty sure I'm re-virginized. He would split me in half with that thing. Maybe I should let him.

No, he's your boss.

"Early bird catches the worm," I say, the pitch of my voice moving higher with each word.

"Just as well, I have a few things I need emailed out today before hair and makeup come for you," he says completely nonchalantly.

I'm thinking about his cock, and he's thinking about work. Obviously, we know who is the sane one in this kitchen.

"Wait?" His last words sink in. "Hair and makeup?"

"Yeah." He slides his cup out from the coffee machine and takes a sip. "I figured you would want both since it's a black-tie gala. Most of the women who attend make a day of it."

"Well, you didn't have to do that, but I'll take advantage of it while it's offered." I walk past him. "I'm going to go drink this on the balcony and then I'll meet you in your office?"

"Take your time."

I'm at the threshold of the door when I hear him call my name. I look over my shoulder and see him smirk at me.

"Better than conventional." He sweeps a hand in front of his body and laughs as I roll my eyes and leave him with his giant ego to keep him company.

The air smells like baking bread as I step outside wrapped in blanket, and my stomach growls. I should have grabbed something from the kitchen, but I couldn't think clearly with all those abs in my face. Had I waited another minute I might have something very different from a croissant in my mouth.

"*Cherie, tu es si belle,*" Helene, the angel sent to do my hair and makeup, says as she clips the chain that holds the back of my dress together. "This dress is magnificent."

"*Merci,*" I say as I run a hand down my body.

The front of the dress has a high neckline, very modest but still somehow so flattering with the boning around the bodice to hold everything in and up. The slit comes to the top of my thigh, the only skin that shows from the front. All the drama is saved for the back, where the dress dips to below my waist.

She gave me a neutral smokey eye and nude lip to keep my makeup subtle. My hair is swept into a low side chignon with a few face framing curls left out. The shoes that Stella chose, adorn my feet and match a small clutch barely big enough for my phone and a lipstick.

Butterflies fill my stomach as I watch Helene pack her things and leave me in the sitting room waiting for Asher. I don't know what to expect. Everything was back to professional when we spent the morning working. He left in the afternoon for a couple hours but didn't tell me where he went.

I look up when I hear a knock on the door frame.

Asher Bennett wearing a suit is handsome. Asher Bennett in gray sweatpants is delicious. But Asher Bennett in a perfectly tailored tuxedo is next level sexy. Every single thing about him is perfectly pieced together, right down to his perfectly tied bowtie.

"You look beautiful," he tells me as I walk toward him, his eye drawn down to the flash of my leg.

"You haven't even seen the best part yet." I turn to show him my back and then look over my shoulder. "Pretty great, huh? Like the mullet of dresses. Business in the front, party in the back."

He smiles at my comparison and runs his finger along his lip. I can always feel the intensity of his gaze, but now it burns through my blood in a completely different way. It feels like he's devouring me with his eyes.

"You are stunning." He reaches into his pocket and pulls out a small box which he hands to me. "These are for you."

My hands shake as I pull the ribbon free and lift the lid. Inside the box are the earrings I tried on at the boutique with the dress. The incredibly expensive earrings, the emeralds and diamonds twinkle in the light of the chandelier.

"Asher, no." I close the lid and try to hand them back. "They're too much."

"I insist." He gently pushes my hand away and moves forward. I look up into his eyes and watch as they soften, and his hard mask disappears. "Tonight, won't be fun for me. There's a lot of tension with my family. Seeing you in these will be a good distraction."

"You play dirty."

"It's the only way to win." He opens the box and holds it up for me. "Put them in and let's go."

I guess I might as well enjoy them while it lasts. I can always tuck them back in his desk on my last day of work. The driver says something to Asher when we step out onto the sidewalk, but I can't understand him, so I just get inside and slide across the bench seat. My entire left leg is exposed due to the slit and goosebumps pebble my skin as the chilly November air drifts into the car.

Asher notices me rubbing my palm over my skin and shrugs out of his jacket, placing it over my lap.

"Thank you," I say as the scent of his cologne fills my nostrils. If I could get away with it, I'd bury my face in the fabric and memorize it. If only it wasn't so inappropriate.

"No problem. It's a fairly short drive, we'll be there in about ten minutes give or take with traffic." He swipes on his phone and pulls up his emails.

I watch as his jaw clenches and unclenches. Right before my eyes he hardens back up. Gone is the man who gently coerced me into wearing these ridiculously priced earrings and in his place is the no bullshit CEO I know so well. At least I know what to expect tonight.

In fact, he mentioned how he'll keep me close all night due to his business dealings while we're at the gala. Apparently last year was his turn to speak at the event, so his family simply expects his presence.

True to his word, we're pulling up to a red carpet with a stand and repeat in less than fifteen minutes.

"You didn't say anything about a red carpet," I look over at him with wide eyes. "I've never done anything remotely like this." I hand him his coat which he sets to the side.

"Don't worry, I've been doing them my entire life. Just follow my lead, and I'll get us off it as fast as possible."

Nausea swirls inside me as the driver opens the door and Asher steps out, first giving the photographers a wave and then turning to help me out. I'm so nervous I stumble, but Asher wraps his arm around me and guides me down the carpet. People call out his name and ask for mine, who I'm wearing, if we're a couple. It's so overwhelming.

Suddenly Asher is in front of me, blocking me from view. His hand cradles my cheek as his looks into my eyes. "Relax, Clara, focus on me and give them that gorgeous, sunny smile of yours. I'm right here with you."

I could kiss him right now. I won't, but I could. "Okay," I say instead.

"I'm going to spin us so they can see the back of this dress and really have something to go wild for. Ready?"

"Yes," I give him a genuine smile and gasp when he really does spin me around. We laugh together as he completely ignores all the questions and focuses entirely on me until we step into the lobby.

Before I can even take a breath, I'm pulled into the arms of Nicolette. "Gorgeous dress, gorgeous entrance. But you need to stop smiling like you have nothing behind your eyes at these events. People will think you're simple."

"Good thing I'll never do one of these again," I say.

"*Non,* I think you have a lot of these in your future. Even now, his eyes follow you from across the lobby where his mother is forcing another woman on him." She gestures with her chin. "Go save him."

When I turn, I find his eyes glued on me, and he motions for me to join him. A thin blonde is standing practically draped around him as he exchanges words with an older woman. She is dressed in a sophisticated navy gown with diamonds dripping off her neck and wrists. Her dark brown hair has streaks of gray, but they look good and only enhance her beauty.

"Mother, this is Clara Snow," he says as he pulls me to his side, anchoring me against him.

"Pleasure to meet you Miss Snow," she says as she holds out her hand. "I've heard a lot about you."

"Thank you. I've enjoyed working for your son. He's a wonderful boss."

Her eyes narrow as they lock on my earrings. "You're just a temp, correct?" Her tone is ice cold.

"I am, yes."

"That'll be enough, Mother." Asher guides me away. "That was probably the most pleasant interaction you'll have with any of my family tonight. Stay close."

"Who was the blonde?" I ask, my voice just a little too tight.

He gives me a knowing look out of the corner of his eye. "I didn't catch her name."

A server walks by with glasses of champagne on a gold tray, and we each grab one. I take a sip, loving the tingle from the bubbles as I swallow.

"Clara," he says as he pulls me closer. "I need you to stay close."

"Taking notes and remembering names for possible investors, I remember." I roll my eyes at the reminder.

"No, because you're my chicken nuggets."

And just like that, Asher Bennett kicked the door to my heart wide open.

CHAPTER 14

ASHER

THE NIGHT WENT WELL on the business front. I made connections with several potential investors from Switzerland and Belgium. Expanding into Europe is so close I can taste it.

Unfortunately, my mother and father spent a good amount of time hassling me and shooting daggers at Clara. I tried my best to deflect them, but I know some barbs hit their mark. I couldn't be prouder of her, though. Even though she doesn't speak any foreign languages, she was able to keep up for the most part.

She's so bright and brave to agree to this. The way she felt in my arms as we moved around the dance floor almost brought me to my knees. Feeling her soft curves pressed against me had me as horny as a teenage boy. And fuck if the skin of her back isn't the silkiest thing I've ever felt. I could barely pull myself away.

She takes her shoes off as soon as we step into the foyer and releases the sexiest fucking moan I've ever heard. I've been sporting a semi for half the night, and just that one noise has my dick perking up even more. I can't hold back any longer. I want her.

I need her.

"Do you want a drink?" I ask as she walks toward her suite.

She stops and smiles over her shoulder at me. "Sure, just let me change first?"

"I'll just be across the hall."

I walk into the living room and pour two glasses of wine.

"Asher?" She's standing in the door, biting her lip. "I can't unclasp the chain on the back of my dress. Can you help me?"

"Of course."

I walk to her as she turns and gives me her back. She's already taken her hair down, so she pulls it to the side. The sight of her back—all the exposed, soft skin I've been salivating over all night—makes any logic fly out the window.

I run my fingers under the chain, not seeing a clasp. "Which side?" I let my fingers run down her spine to the edge of the dress which sits just above her ass.

"The left," she says as she moves her arm out of the way. "It's under the material of the dress, sewn into seam."

I follow her directions, barely holding back a moan of

my own when the chain comes free, and I see a brief glimpse of the curve of her breast. My hands move down to her hips, and I press my lips to the back of her neck where it meets her shoulder.

She tenses with a sharp intake of breath.

"I'm sorry." I immediately release her and step back. "That was out of line."

"No." She turns, clutching her loosened dress to her chest. "It's not that I don't want...that I'm not interested." A crease forms between her eyebrows. "Because I definitely am, but I don't think it's a good idea. You're my boss."

"No, you're right." I try to smile, but it's more a grimace. "Let's blame it on the champagne."

"Okay, good." She nods as if she's trying to convince herself. "That's good. No harm, no foul."

"Right." I take a drink of wine.

"I'm going to go to bed. I'm more tired than I thought I was."

"Good night."

"Night." She disappears from the room leaving nothing but that addictive orange and vanilla scent of hers and a raging hard on tenting my trousers.

I yank my bowtie off and start unbuttoning my shirt as I walk down the hall toward my room. I can't believe I did that without first asking her. What kind of creep am I? I'll be lucky if she doesn't hit me with a lawsuit. Nico is going to flip his shit.

As I'm pulling my shirt out of my pants and about to close my door behind me, I hear footsteps. I turn to see

Clara, still clutching her dress to her chest. I lean against the door frame and unbuckle my belt, slowly pulling it through the loops. Her eyes watch my movements until we're face to face.

"Clara?" I raise an eyebrow as I wait for her to speak.

"Maybe," she begins, licking her lips nervously, "maybe we should get it out of our systems."

I don't think one night with her would get it out of my system if I'm being painfully honest with myself. A huge change from what I'm used to.

"What happens in Paris, stays in Paris," she continues nervously.

"Wrong city for that phrase."

Her face falls at my answer.

"But I'll take tonight. Drop that dress and tell me you want this as much as I do."

Her eyes meet mine in a clash of steely resolve as she lets the dress drop to the floor leaving her completely nude aside from the earrings I gave her.

"I want this as much as you do."

Before she can even take a breath, I'm on her. My mouth slants over hers as I drink from her soft, full lips. I walk us back into my room as she pushes my shirt off my shoulders. My fingers dive into her hair, pulling on the roots and tilting her head back so I can deepen our kiss.

"Were you this naked under your dress all night?" I ask against her lips.

"Yes." She runs her hands from my shoulders down my chest and abs to my waist. "I almost begged for this when you walked in the kitchen this morning," she confesses as she grinds her pelvis against mine.

I kick the door closed behind me and nudge her down on the edge of my bed. "Lie back."

She rests back on her elbows and watches me as I lower to my knees and spread her knees apart. She's already wet for me and lets her head drop back as I glide my thumb along her slit. Her hips rock against me as I tease her with gentle strokes. When I've driven her to the edge, I cover her with my mouth.

She moans my name as I circle my tongue around her tiny, throbbing clit. Fuck, she tastes good. I slip my tongue inside her, swirling and plunging until I feel her fingers tugging on my hair. I move back to her clit and slide two fingers inside her, hooking them upward to find her g-spot.

I stay down there, determined to taste her orgasm before even considering my own pleasure. Her thighs shake and tighten around my head, but I keep my steady pace going. I can't help but smile as she cries out, clenching around me and drenching my lips and chin in her release. I lap and lick and suck until all her orgasm tremors subside.

"I've wanted to do that since we were standing in your kitchen," I confess as I stand and push up to where her head is on the pillows. "Better than anything I could have hoped for."

CHAPTER 15

CLARA

HE CRAWLS UP MY BODY, stopping to lavish attention on each of my nipples using his hands and mouth. His hand moves over my stomach to my waist. If that move is anything to go by, he isn't put off by my bigger than what he's used to body. It makes it that much sexier as his lips move up my chest, up my neck, and back to my lips.

I love that I can taste myself on him. But I want more. I want to taste him. I reach down and push the rest of his clothes down his legs. His cock bounces free, and I'll be goddamned if it isn't even bigger than I thought.

I wrap my hand around him and pump, gathering the precum on the tip and smearing it around his crown. I roll us so he's on his back and a laugh slips from his lips.

"Eager little thing, aren't you?" he asks as he adjusts his

position to watch. "Suck my cock," he commands, and fuck if it doesn't make me want to do as he says.

I take the tip into my mouth and lave my tongue all around it. I look up into his eyes as I take him as deep as I can, bottoming out when his crown hits the back of my throat. His cock jerks inside my mouth.

"Fuck," he whispers as I increase my pace. Up and down his cock, sucking and licking as he thickens inside my mouth. He grabs my hair to still me, "I'm going to cum."

I appreciate his warning but cover his hand with mine and keeping going until he finishes. I swallow every earthy, salty bit he gives me, licking him clean as he catches his breath. I move back up to lay beside him, but he pulls me on top instead.

"I want to watch you ride me," he says. His hands move over my belly and cup my breasts. He teases my nipples and my pussy comes to life all over again. But surely, he isn't able to go again so soon.

"Don't you need a break to catch your breath?" I ask as I rock my hips back and forth.

"No," he lifts my hips the slightest bit and presses his cock at my entrance. He drags the tip along my folds, teasing my clit and making me crazy with need. "Feel that? That's what you do to me. I could spend all night fucking you and never lose it."

He slips inside me, slowly lowering me onto his length. Every inch stretches me further and further until I don't think I can take it any longer. I feel so full. So treasured.

I begin to move my hips back and forth, taking him

deeper and deeper. His lips part as he watches me move and his fingertips dig into my flesh, urging me to go harder and deeper. I feel heat build deep within me as he circles his thumb over my clit in quick and precise strokes. I cry out as I clench around him and heat tears through my body.

He flips us around so I'm on my back once again, and he lifts my right leg over his shoulder. Both of his hands grip my hips, and he thrusts into me over and over. All the muscles of his abs are flexed as he drives me toward another unbelievable peak of passion.

"One more. Give me one more," he moans between thrusts. "Fuck, you feel perfect. Come for me again."

As if my body is his to command, I shatter around him again. He holds me still as his cock thickens inside me, but at the last minute, he pulls out. Thick ropes of his cum land on my belly and thighs, and he grips his base so hard his knuckles turn white. He slumps down beside me and rubs his cum into my skin.

"Mine," he says possessively as he pulls me into his arms.

"Do you need anything?" I ask, unsure of how this part goes. Should I go back to my room? Are we done here?

"Yeah, for you to rest so I can do that to you over and over again."

"Okay." I roll away from him and start to stand.

"Whoa." He grabs me by the waist and hauls me back against him. "Where do you think you're going?"

"To bed."

"You're in bed."

"Your bed."

"That's right. My bed that I invited you into. Lay back down."

I settle back in his arms, rolling to face him. He presses his lips to my forehead as his hands move up and down my back, easing my nerves with each caress. This side of him, the soft and gentle side buried beneath his cold businessman exterior is so unexpected.

"This feels good," he mumbles sleepily.

It does. It feels too good.

Asher wanted me to go home with him tonight but after being gone for a few days I needed to get back to see Steve. I gave Maria my keys to clean his litter box and make sure he had enough food and water, but I've never been away from him for this long before.

He's laying in a bowl I store above my kitchen cabinet when I walk in the door. I push my suitcase to the side and look up at him. It's his favorite position, lording over his lowly human. His yellow eyes slowly move to me before he flips and gives me his back.

"I bet you a bag of catnip I'll wake up in the morning to find you cuddled up beside me, you furry little demon." All I get in response to that comment is a twitching ear as I leave to go down to the restaurant and pick up my key.

It's a slow night, so Maria walks right over to wear I'm sitting at the end of the bar. She slings a towel over her shoulder and places a basket of chips and some salsa down in front of me. I ask for a water before digging in.

"How was your trip?" she asks as she sets it down on a coaster.

My cheeks heat as I pause with a chip halfway to my mouth. "Good."

She narrows her eyes, obviously knowing I'm full of shit.

I shove the chip in my mouth and give her a closed mouth smile as I chew. "How was Steve? Did he behave for you?"

"More than you are. What happened on your trip? Where did you even go?"

"I went to Paris for work," I finally answer. "I only saw a few landmarks, just the highlights really, otherwise I was working." Partial truth, partial lie. Asher did take me by Notre Dame, we couldn't go inside, and obviously the restoration work was ongoing, but it was still so incredibly beautiful.

Her eyes turn wistful. "I've always wanted to go to Paris. The closest I've gotten is walking around the Paris casino in Vegas."

"It's beautiful. In the morning the air smells like baking bread." And car exhaust but that's any big city.

I get a text while I'm finishing up dinner. It's a picture of the skyline from some high-rise along the river.

Asher: You'd look good pressed against this window

Clara: I look better sitting here, eating my weight in chips and salsa and tacos al pastor.

I send him a quick selfie.

Asher: Bring your tacos
Clara: What about Steve?
Asher: Bring him too

Is he serious?

Clara: He's upset with me. Wouldn't move from his position as overlord of the apartment.
Asher: Can't blame a guy for missing you
Clara: Am I being pranked?
Clara: What are we even doing here?

I thought for sure this would be over once the plane touched down.

Asher: I don't know

I didn't reply after that, and I spend the rest of the evening alone on the receiving end of a cat's cold shoulder.

CHAPTER 16

ASHER

I'VE AMASSED a creepy number of photos of Clara over the past month. I think about her last text to me as I flip through them ending with the one I snapped this morning before she woke up. Her long, shiny brown hair had the most brilliant shades of red in the early morning sunlight. The way her legs parted for me as she was just waking and how good it felt to slip inside her, fucking her softly as she woke.

I've never been a morning sex person. Fuck, I've never wanted to wake up next to someone else in general. But as I slow my pace on the treadmill, I realize that I do want that. I want that with *her*.

She thinks that this weekend was just us getting caught up in the moment. The excitement of her trip to Paris mixed with the grandeur of the gala. It makes sense that in her mind it was a one off. The circumstances too extravagant to be real or meaningful.

I pick up my phone and text the only person who could help me with this.

Asher: I need your help
Stella: What else is new?
Asher: Ha
Asher: But seriously, what can I do to show someone I'm not just a weekend fuck?

I sound needy.

Stella: Whoa
Stella: Who are we talking about here?
Asher: I'd rather not say at this juncture in the relationship
Stella: Ash
Asher: Stella
Stella: Fine.
Stella: If it's who I think it is, you're going to have to stay yourself but with less flash and money. Think football Sunday vibes. Casual, kicked back.
Stella: Private jets and fine jewelry are great, but she has substance

She's absolutely right. You don't have to know Clara for long to see the depth of her character. She knew almost every employees' name within a week, including the janitorial staff. She stops to help everyone she comes across. If serving others while remaining inconspicuous was an Olympic sport, she'd have more golds than Michael Phelps.

Stella: And for the record, she knows you aren't just a weekend fuck.
Asher: Don't tell Nico about this conversation

He'd never let me live it down if he knew I called myself a weekend fuck.

Stella: I'll keep your secrets
Stella: I'm taking your girl to the party planner's warehouse today. We're picking all the decor for the holiday party.
Asher: She'll love that

I don't even bother correcting the assertion of Clara being mine because she is. She just doesn't know it yet.

Every time I hear the elevator open, I can't stop my eyes from darting to see if it's Clara getting off. I wonder what she did last night. What type of festive monstrosity she'll come in wearing. It's an addictive game, trying to figure out her next move.

After being disappointed by Nico and then Taylor's appearances, I'm rewarded with the sight that I've been craving for the past fourteen hours. Clara walks in with candy cane striped leggings under an oversize black sweater. On anyone else, the ensemble would look ridiculous, but on her it works. Or maybe I'm just obsessed.

She studiously avoids eye contact with me as she pulls her scarf off and hangs it beside her coat. She speaks quietly with Taylor and Tory, sharing smiles with them. Then she pulls a small box out of her purse and walks to my office.

"May I come in?" she asks from the threshold.

"Of course." I hit the button to turn the glass from clear to frosted. "Close the door behind you." It's not out of the ordinary for me to change the glass throughout the workday, especially if I'm talking one-on-one to someone. "Lock it."

She pauses with her back to me, her hand on the knob. "Asher," she says my name quietly. "We can't."

"It's my company, we can do whatever the fuck I want. What's in your hand?"

She turns and looks from me to the box. "I picked this up for you in Paris." She stands on the other side of the desk holding it out to me.

"Come over here and hand it to me." I push back from the desk, staying in my chair but making room for her.

"This feels like a trap." She fights a smile as she comes to a stop in front of me.

I grab her wrist as she offers the box and pull her onto my lap. "Much better."

She tenses briefly but then relaxes into my hold. "Open it."

I give her a look as I untie the string holding the box together. "You didn't have to get me anything."

"The irony of that statement coming from those lips."

"I'm open to suggestions if you'd like me to make other things come from these lips."

"Doesn't TechJet have a policy about fraternization?"

"Consider it terminated," I say as I pull the lid off the box.

Inside, tucked into a bed of tissue paper is a small snow globe. The Eiffel Tower stands in the middle of the city with a Santa hat sitting askew atop it. It's kitschy and quirky and exactly what I'd expect to receive from her.

"I saw it when I was out walking the morning of the gala. It just felt right."

She feels right.

"Thank you, I love it." I set it on my desk and pull her face to mine.

Her lips part as I cover them with my own. I kiss her softly, slowly, and deeply as her fingers run through my hair. Every pass of her tongue against mine sends waves of warmth within me. I could happily drown in her.

She moans against my mouth as my hand travels up her thigh to cup her over her leggings. Fuck, I wish she was wearing just a dress. I can feel the heat of her pussy and knowing how good she feels all hot and wet for me drives me to the brink of insanity.

She pulls away with a gasp, her hands on my shoulders and eyes glazed with desire. "We should stop. Stella said we'd be leaving early today, and I haven't even ordered your breakfast yet."

"It's okay, I'd rather have you for breakfast."

She laughs.

But I'm serious.

She sobers. "Are you serious?"

"Yes. The thought of laying you across this desk and devouring that sweet pussy makes me rock-fucking-hard." I guide her hand over my dick, straining against the material of my pants.

"You're worse than a teenager."

"Trust me, I know."

"I thought this was just a Paris thing?" Her eyes move back and forth between mine.

"Should I call my pilots?"

"No." She huffs a laugh and rests her forehead against mine. "This could be messy. We need rules."

"Okay," I say as I lean back, reaching for a legal pad to write on. "First rule?"

"No funny business at work."

I raise an eyebrow and look at her before writing. "Rule number one, no funny business at work." I have a pretty good idea of what she means by 'funny business' but I'm not going to press for details because, loopholes.

"Two, no one can know until I no longer work here."

"Stella knows. Or at least suspects." I tap the pen against my lip as I think.

"You told her?" Clara looks genuinely surprised.

"No, but she's known me forever and is highly perceptive, with few exceptions." Like her thoughts about Nico. "Rule three," I say as I continue to write, "this is an exclusive arrangement."

She nods in agreement.

"Anything else before we sign and date?"

"I can't think of anything." She grabs the pen and signs her name and writes the date. "We can always write addendums."

"Better watch out, that kind of dirty talk might make me want to break rule number one." I start to move my hand up her sweater.

"No breaking the rules," she squeals.

We're both laughing when we hear a knock on the door. Clara scrambles off my lap and back around the desk, motioning for me to wipe her lipstick off my mouth. She turns and opens the door to Nico standing in the way, scowling at me.

"Sorry," Clara says as she sidesteps him. "I have no idea how that locked." She sends me a worried look over her shoulder after she leaves the office, but I lose sight of her as the door closes.

CHAPTER 17

CLARA

"THIS IS the most magical place I've ever seen," I say as I walk through the fourth themed room of a large holiday warehouse.

Stella brought me here to look through themed holiday decor for the party in December. We've been through a red room, a green room, a blue and silver room, and now white, gold, and silver. The party specialist is talking about all the boring details with Stella while I wander around and salivate over the trees.

We've walked through three dozen different setups by the time the specialist leaves us in a conference room with two cups of spiced cider to make our choice. My feet are killing me, but the smile I've been wearing feels like it is permanently etched onto my face.

"I don't want to see another Christmas tree until I'm ninety years old," Stella groans. "How are you still so excited?"

"Don't you feel it? The way the Christmas spirit wraps you in a hug in the warmth of the soft lights of all the trees. Nothing makes me happier."

Stella looks at me as if I've gone a little mad and separates the information sheets for each room into yes and no piles based on price. "Here, choose from these. I don't care which you go with, but we have to keep in mind we'll still have food and beverage to pay for with our budget."

I flip through the pages and decide on the white, sliver, and gold snow theme. Classic color choices with a modern twist. It feels very Asher and, in turn, very TechJet. Plus, somehow, I just know having understated decor will make him less of a Scrooge.

"I think we should go with this one." I slide the sheet to her.

"Good choice, it was one of my favorites. Very chic." She stands and takes it over to finalize details. She walks back over when she's finished and taps a nail on the table. "Do you want to go have dinner and a drink tonight? I could use some girl talk."

"Sure, that sounds great." Honestly, I could use some too.

We end up at a trendy sushi bar that you usually have to have reservations for weeks in advance but somehow Stella gets us a table as walk-ins. Her phone lights up with missed calls and texts from Nico, but she ignores them as she peruses the menu.

"Is everything okay?" I gesture to her phone as another missed call shows up.

She sighs and glances at it. "We got into an argument this morning. It seems to be happening more and more."

"I'm sorry to hear that. He did look exceptionally pissed this morning when I left Asher's office. I thought it was just because the door was locked." I take a sip of my cocktail.

"Why was it locked?" A wicked smile crosses her face.

"Nothing tawdry," I say as my cheeks heat.

"Really?"

I use my cocktail as a shield and nod after taking a sip.

"Damn, because I think you'd be amazing for him." She takes a drink. "He's stubborn and an asshole and so fucking serious all the time. Don't get me wrong, I love him like I love my own brothers, but he needs someone to breathe life into him."

"Even if we were together, I don't see how I would help. I'm just a temp, I'll be gone as quick as I appeared."

"Why a temp?" She leans forward over the table. "Everyone has seen how competent you are in everything you do. Hell, you're above and beyond competent. It's like you've been here from the beginning. The entire company misses Sara, but they'll miss you just as much."

"That's very kind." And likely an exaggeration. "I guess I fell into being a temp because it gives me the freedom to volunteer. I don't worry about taking work home with me."

She studies me over the rim of her glass with skepticism

shining in her eyes but thankfully lets it go. "Tell me about Paris. Did Ash let you have any time to sight see?"

"Yes," I answer with a big smile. "We stopped one night after dinner and walked around the Eiffel Tower. I have pictures." I open my phone and slide it over to her.

I watch as she scrolls through them amused and then surprise flickers across her face.

"What?" I ask, alarmed.

She holds the phone out to me, it's one that Asher airdropped to me. We're holding each other and smiling so wide that his dimple has popped out. I'm looking at him with stars in my eyes.

"He never smiles like this in photos." Her eyes water when they meet mine. "I've never seen him look so happy."

"It was a candid. I think we were actually insulting each other when that was taken." The back of my eyes sting with the emotion in hers.

"I don't care," she says as she hands the phone back to me. "If you keep making him smile like that I'll stay out of your business. But that," she points her fork at my phone, "is exactly what I was talking about."

I look down at the photo again, tiny seeds of hope taking root inside me. Maybe this could be real.

"Are you ready for this?" I ask Asher as we walk into the shelter an hour before Thanksgiving service starts.

"Does it matter if I say no?"

"Nope." I reach into my bag and take out two stuffed turkey hats and hand him one. "We're wearing these over our hair nets."

He takes one look and shakes his head vehemently. "Absolutely not."

"Please." I give him puppy dog eyes and put mine on. "I'm wearing mine."

"You're also wearing a sweater with a picture of two cartoon turkey legs that says, 'I'm a leg man.' Your judgement is skewed."

"Hey, this sweater was my best find of my last thrifting trip." I bump his hip and smile up at him. I'm so glad he followed through.

"I can't wait to get it off you." He fists my ponytail and steals a kiss. "Thank you for agreeing to spend the night with me tonight."

He said he had something planned just for the two of us. His parents are out of the country still and while he could have spent the holiday with his brothers, or even Stella or Nico, he wanted to be with me.

"Happy Thanksgiving," Daniel, the shelter director, says as he approaches us.

I release my hold on Asher and move into Daniel's open arms for a quick hug.

"Daniel, this is my friend Asher. Asher, this is Daniel, the guy in charge."

Asher's face has hardened into his professional mask as he shakes Daniel's hand, and I worry that I said something wrong. I don't have time to ask because Daniel assigns us to our tasks. Asher will be scooping mashed potatoes, and I'll be serving pie.

I keep a close eye on Asher as he settles into his roll once the line opens. His expression softens more and more with each person who he serves, but the children in line are where his compassion really shines. My heart bursts as I watch him sneak an extra scoop to a little boy trailing behind his mother and younger sister.

The more time I spend with him, the more I see him. He's had to grow a thick exterior to be as successful as he is without the support of his family. None of them believed in him. Even with privileges of growing up wealthy that type of emotional neglect still hurts. It's why he clings so tight to Stella and Nico. They're more of a family than anything I've come close to experiencing.

"Do you have a minute?" Daniel asks as we close down the line so the volunteers can eat, too.

"Sure thing."

"I have a date for the presentation. The committeeman finally got back to us."

"Oh, great!" I notice Asher sitting at a table with John, one of our regulars. "When will it be?"

"Christmas Eve at eleven in the morning." He follows me to a table and sits down across from me. "I have to admit, running a shelter is one thing, but I feel out of my depth because they asked for a business plan and several other things I don't have ready yet."

"Do you have a list of what they want?"

"Yeah." He pulls out his phone. "I have an email I could forward you."

I spend a few minutes looking over what they asked for from him, and I'm immediately irritated. This is a charity shelter, not a Fortune 500 business. I can already see the red tape they're throwing up straight from the outset. If we're going to make this work, it'll take a lot of work between now and then.

CHAPTER 18

ASHER

MY EYES WANDER to Clara as she sits with the shelter director. They're bent over their phones and look to be discussing something in depth. Part of me wants to go insert myself. To wrap my arm around her in a wordless claim, but I push that baser instinct to the side.

Instead, I find myself sitting across from an older gentleman who looks to be about my father's age. Deep lines mar the weathered skin of his face, but despite his circumstances he looks strong and healthy. Not for the first time today, I find myself wondering what forced these people into their current situations. Not in judgement, just curiosity.

"You're new here," the man across from me says with a deep baritone.

"Yeah, I came with Clara."

He turns his head and looks at her. "She's good people."

"The best," I agree. "I'm Asher." I hold my hand out.

"Jack." He takes mine and shakes firmly. "How do you know Clara?"

"Apparently I'm her *friend*." The word tastes as bitter on my tongue as it sounds to my ears.

He chuckles and dunks a piece of his turkey into the pale gravy. "What's your line of work? Seems like you do something fancy by the look of you."

"I run a tech startup."

"I was never one for all that." He scoops another bite into his mouth. "Although for a while I did run my own business."

"Oh yeah?" I'm genuinely interested in his story. It's jarring to imagine owning a business and then ending up homeless.

"Yep. Ran a construction business about twenty-five years ago. Was doing real well with it until I won a contract over a big development firm. Bastards never let go, so when I fell on hard times after a lawsuit, they swooped in and bought me out. A few months later my wife was diagnosed with cancer. I spent all my savings on trying to get her the medical help she needed, but in the end it was too late. I was so deep in medical debt I lost the house and car."

"I'm so sorry."

"Not your fault. I started drinking and couldn't hold a job. I've bounced around a lot, sometimes finding work but often not. I bounce between shelters and sometimes finding a cheap apartment for a few months ever since."

The wheels in my mind start turning. I'm sure dad could find a job for him somewhere within the company. If Jack was even amenable to it.

"You working now?"

"No, just odds and ends around here for Daniel. Sometimes I'll fix something at home for some of the other staff and volunteers. Nothing regular."

"I might have a connection for you, if you're interested."

"Sure. Ten years ago I would have been too prideful to take you up on that. But now, I'll take anything I can."

"What's the best way to reach you?"

"Reach out to Clara or Daniel, they can usually track me down."

I watch him get up and throw his trash away, disappearing into the cold, gray Chicago afternoon. On the scale of things I want to do, asking my father for a favor ranks right up there with a colonoscopy, but something inside me says I need to do this. I need to help, even if it's just a little push, a small connection.

I stand and clear what's left on the now empty table, taking it back into the kitchen and handing it off to the volunteers on cleanup. When I walk back out, I see Clara, deep in discussion with Daniel still. Her bright smile was filling the room with sunshine all day until she sat down to eat with him.

"What's going on?" I ask as I pull out a chair beside her.

"Daniel's trying to acquire the other half of the block to expand the shelter and asked me to help when he goes to make his presentation for the zoning committee."

"After weeks of run-around they finally gave me an appointment." He pushes his hair off his forehead, looking stressed. "Clara knows this business stuff better than me."

"Look at what they want from him." She slides a phone in front of me. "This is a charity, not a business. It's absolutely absurd."

Some requests are warranted but others are borderline unreasonable. I look at the name of the committeeman they're dealing with and my stomach sours. He's a friend of my father's and a morally corrupt piece of trash.

"I could help you with a few things on this list." Any chance to stick it to these old fucks is a chance I'll take. I loathe ninety-five percent of the people in my parents' social circle.

"Really?" Clara looks at me wide-eyed. "You think you have time?"

"I can make time," I say, a little offended that she's so surprised.

"That would be so fantastic," Daniel agrees enthusiastically. "I'll take any help I can get here. We're not affiliated with a big church; we don't have massive donors. It's just the people you see here in this building that keep the shelter running. We're always grateful for any help we can get."

We chat for a few more minutes while we wait for Tom to bring the car around. I pull Clara into my arms and duck around the side of the building, pressing her against the wall and attacking her mouth with mine.

"Do you kiss all your friends like that?" I ask when we break apart.

"I didn't know what to call you." She grips the lapels of my jacket and pulls me down for another kiss. "We haven't defined the relationship."

"We signed a contract."

"So," she pauses to press a wet, open mouth kiss to my neck, "business partners?"

I grab her wrists and pin them above her head. "You're mine."

"Guess that makes you mine then, too."

"I wouldn't do this for anyone but you," I cover her mouth again. My tongue slides against hers as she arches her body into mine. "I have a surprise for you, tonight."

"It better not be expensive and over-the-top." She bites my lip and tugs gently.

"Pot meet kettle. You're the most wonderfully over-the-top person I've ever met." I smile down at her, loving the soft look in her eyes and the rosy glow of her cheeks as she smiles back. My phone alerts me to Tom's arrival, so I grab her hand and pull her around to the front of the building again.

This oven is my nemesis. I own a tech company and cannot for the life of me figure out how to turn on this godforsaken appliance. Note to self, never buy European appliances again.

I told Clara to go take a nice long bath while I fix our dinner. She mentioned the other day over dinner that it's the one thing her apartment lacks that she wishes she had. Luckily for both of us, I have a deep tub just waiting here in my place for her.

I finally break down and text Stella asking for instructions on the oven. She has the same one and is the only one who has ever used mine. She'll never let me live this down, but it's worth it. I want Clara to know she's safe with me, so I'm making her the comfort meal she told me about in Paris.

I finally get the oven started—thank you, Stella—and slide a baking sheet with chicken nuggets into the oven. Then I put some fries in the air fryer while I clean some berries. I'm plating everything as she walks into the kitchen.

My mouth goes dry at the sight of her. She's wearing one of my dress shirts that hits her at mid-thigh. Her legs and feet are bare, and her hair is piled on top of her head. I can't form words for a moment as all I can think is how much I need to feel her. But, first, I need her to understand the depth of my feelings. How much I care for her. I dig deep for my composure.

"Go ahead and sit at the table," I tell her before she sees what I've got. "How was your bath?"

"Incredible. I'll be over here all the time now."

"Consider it available at your beck and call." I take two glasses of Chardonnay and set them on the table before going back for the plates.

She makes a strangled sound when she notices what I'm placing in front of her. Then she's completely silent, her eyes trained on the plate in front of her. Worry starts to claw at my chest. Maybe I miscalculated this meal.

My stomach drops when I see the first tear roll down her cheek.

CHAPTER 19

CLARA

HEAT BURNS my eyes as I hold them open, staring at the food placed in front of me. Everything blurs as the first few tears escape. I can barely breathe, my chest is tight, and my throat is clogged with emotion. With gratitude.

This man who I truly once thought hated me, has not only listened to me but *heard* me. I finally look up at him, tears rolling down my face and grab his hands. I open my mouth to speak, but no words form.

I can't make out his facial expression because everything is so blurry, but he cups my cheek and wipes some of the tears with his thumbs. He begins to apologize, but I shake my head as I lean into his touch. I press my lips to his palm and sob.

"Clara, I'm sorry. I just wanted to make this for you so

you would know that I want to be your safe space. I want to be someone you can count on and turn to and trust."

"I know," I finally manage to choke out. "I'm not upset. I'm touched so deeply." I draw a shuddering breath. "I've lived nearly my entire life never feeling safe or cared for by other people. I don't know how to process these feelings."

I feel like I'm flying and falling all at once. The magnitude of this gesture and the feelings that go along with it are overpowering in the purest way. All my defense mechanisms are failing me here and now. I can't think a thought to deflect or make a joke to change the subject, I can't even stop the flow of tears from my eyes. They fall for younger me, who never got to experience this feeling. They fall for future me because nothing in my life ever lasts. All my experiences and relationships have been fleeting, and now I can't help but start falling for him.

Asher lifts me into his arms from the chair and walks us into his living room. He settles onto the couch with me straddling his legs, my face tucked against his neck. His hands run up and down my back in long soothing strokes while he lets me cry it all out.

When I finally get myself under control, I drag in a deep breath and sit back. Looking into his deep green eyes I see nothing but concern and affection reflected back in. He reaches up and wipes the remainders of the tears from my cheeks with his thumbs.

"If you didn't want to eat my cooking, all you had to do was say so." The statement is delivered with such sincerity that I almost think he's serious, until his lip curves in a smirk.

"Were you working hard on those nuggets while I took a bath?"

"I was actually," he mutters. "Are you okay? I really had no idea you'd react like that."

"I didn't either. I'm okay. More than okay."

I take his face in my hands and pull him to me for a kiss. It is slow at first, just my lips moving over his, our tongues lightly stroking each other's until his fingers find my hips and drag me up his thighs. I can feel his cock hardening against my center as I rock my hips, seeking friction.

His fingers deftly work the buttons of the shirt I borrowed. I grab the hem of his shirt and pull it over his head as soon as he has the buttons undone. He doesn't push his shirt off my shoulders. Instead, he draws his finger down the exposed line of flesh from lips, down my neck, through the valley of my breasts, over the outward curve of my belly. Goosebumps follow his finger and heat begins to build in my core.

"You are so beautiful," he says quietly as he moves his palm back up my body until he's cupping my breast. He twists my nipple and then circles it until it hardens into a stiff peak. His mouth lowers to the rosy bud and takes it between his lips, circling it with his tongue.

My fingers move through the silky hard strands of his hair as I hold him close. He grabs my other hand and lowers it between my legs, sliding my fingers along my wet slit.

"Touch yourself," he commands before moving onto my other breast.

I immediately follow his order, finding my clit and teasing it as my body becomes heavy with need. He finally pushes the shirt off my shoulders leaving me fully nude in his lap. He leans back against the couch to give himself a better view of me working myself.

"Fuck yourself." Another command that has me whimpering as my fingers slide back and into my wet channel. He shifts his hand down to my hip and drags his thumb over my clit. "You're so beautiful. Work that pussy for me. I want to hear how wet and desperate you are for me."

My gaze stays locked on his face while he watches my fingers. A moan slips from my lips as I watch his part, his tongue running slowly along his full bottom lip. I've never touched myself like this in front of anyone and it feels dirty but so, so right.

"Tell me what you feel, Sunshine. Let me know what my cock is missing while your fingers are buried in that cunt."

"Wet," I whisper tentatively.

"Go on."

"Hot and soft."

"Keeping going," he rasps, circling my clit harder now.

"Fuck, Ash." My walls begin to spasm around my fingers. "I'm going to cum."

"Good girl, Sunshine. Let go, I want to watch."

I find my g-spot and between his fingers and mine the orgasm crashes over me. His hands move to my hips, gripping them as I ride my fingers through the final waves of my release. My breathing is still erratic as he slides his fingers under my bun and pulls my head down to his.

The kiss is hard and lustful, a clash of tongues and lips fighting for control. I reach down and fumble with his pants. I need to feel him inside me. He lifts his hips to help maneuver them down his thighs.

His cock springs free, standing angry between us. I run my fist over him from root to tip, loving the way he jerks and twitches at my touch. I gather the bead of pre-cum on his tip with my thumb and slowly bring it to my mouth.

He watches as I lick my thumb, desire darkening his eyes. I feel him cup my breasts again, pinching each nipple hard enough to skate the line of pleasure and pain.

"Ride me," he commands, pulling me closer and then reaching between us as I hold onto his shoulders. He drags the tip of his cock along my slit, teasing me with his proximity. Then he places his crown at my entrance, waiting for me.

I lower myself slowly, savoring each inch that I sink. He fills me so good, like we're two puzzle pieces that belong together. I glide up and down his length keeping the same torturously slow pace as we watch where we're joined. He looks up into my eyes and then his lips descend on mine. He wraps an arm around me and stands, still sheathed inside me.

"I need you in my bed."

He carries me into the bedroom as I press my lips to his neck with tiny, soft kisses. I'm set down on the edge of the bed, and my legs are pushed apart. For a moment I feel bereft without him but then he lowers to the floor between and covers my pussy with mouth. I fall back onto the cool sheets as his tongue lashes against my clit. He flicks it, then circles it, over and over again as my toes curl painfully.

His fingers slide inside me, following the same rhythm as his mouth, driving me closer and closer to the edge. I pull him closer with my heels digging into his shoulders. As soon as I feel the edge of my release crescendo, he stops, stands, and slams his cock inside me.

It's so deep and so hard I see stars. The sheets fist in my hands as he pumps inside me. I wrap a leg around his waist trying to get him deeper. My orgasm explodes within me, the shockwaves and heat radiating from my core in trembling waves of pleasure.

He pumps once, twice, three more times before staying buried deep inside me. His chest rising and falling deeply as I feel him surge within me with his release. He wraps his arm around me and pulls us both up onto the bed properly, all while staying inside me, where he collapses half on top of me.

A few minutes of silence go by before he pulls out and walks off into the bathroom. I hear the sink run and he comes back out with a damp washcloth. The warmth soothes some of the ache away as he cleans me up.

I'm half asleep when he slides between the sheets next to me. He wraps me in his arms and kisses my forehead. "Goodnight, Sunshine."

"You know what this place needs?" I say as I sit at Asher's kitchen island sipping coffee and eating breakfast. "A Christmas tree."

I look around the stark kitchen and living room areas. So clinically designed. No personal touches at all. It looks like he pointed at a catalog and bought everything on the page.

He arches a brow at me. "Why? It's just me here most of the time."

"Because it's Christmas. Because it'll warm this cold space up. I've seen mannequins with more personality than this apartment."

"It's not that bad," he says before sipping his coffee.

Like the regimented, stick in the mud he can be, he wanted to order breakfast from his usual place. The only difference is that instead of one of his sexy suits he's in sexier sweatpants and no shirt. Those delicious glasses are perched on his nose, too.

"What are you doing today?" I ask him.

"Hopefully you." He looks up from his phone with a cheeky grin. "A dozen more times."

"That can be arranged." I lean over and give him a kiss. "After we go get you a tree."

"I don't have decorations."

I smile wider. "Another thing to add to the list."

He groans.

"Please?" I lean my head against his shoulder.

"On one condition."

"Anything."

"I want you to spend more nights here."

"I can't leave Steve."

"I already bought a litter box and a cat tree for him. Tell me what food he likes, and I'll get that, too."

"When did you buy all that?"

"This morning when I woke up next to you and realized I want it every day."

How am I supposed to say no to that?

"Dirty talking in the bedroom. Sweet talking at the breakfast table. What's next?"

"Wait and see." He kisses my nose and walks off.

CHAPTER 20

ASHER

IN ALL THIRTY-TWO years of my life, I've never set foot on a Christmas tree farm. I'm ninety-nine percent sure I've actually never set foot on any farm, at least since I was old enough to remember. The first snow of the season fell last night, I watched as the first fat flakes started floating past the windows while Clara slept on my chest.

Winter has always been my favorite season in Chicago. Most hate the icy wind coming off the lake and sometimes endless snow, but I love the brutality of it. The fight between nature and civilization. The way the city feels so quiet with a fresh layer of snow and glitters with ice.

"I've never been to a Christmas tree farm before," Clara says from beside me in my SUV. She has a leg tucked under her as she sips a peppermint mocha.

"Me either." I smile over at her.

"We're sharing a first?" She beams back at me, stealing my breath with how gorgeous and happy she looks. "I think that will be a rare occurrence for us."

"You think so?"

"Yeah, I mean, how could it not? You are so much more worldly than me. So much access to things I never in my wildest dreams dreamt of."

"What are some things on that list?"

"Wildest dreams?" She taps on her lip and thinks. "Travel, in general. There are so many things to see in the world, but I'd love to travel around the Mediterranean. See everything from Egypt to Spain. I've always been obsessed with history. Maybe it's because I know so little of my own."

"Do you want to know more? You could take one of those DNA tests."

"I've thought about it. I always stop myself, though, because what if I'm matched with my father. What if he has a family and I come along and ruin it? Or worse, what if he's dead like my mom, or in prison? The truth could be worse than knowing."

I don't know what to say to that because she's right, he could be anyone. It's hard for me to put myself in her shoes. I know my family history on both sides going back generations. I know the village in France my mom's family is from. I know my dad's side of the family has been firmly planted in Illinois since after the civil war.

"If you ever change your mind and want to find out, I'll

be there for you." I place my hand on her thigh and squeeze, my fingers inside a tear in her jeans.

"What about you?" she asks. "Anything you haven't done that you want to?"

A family of my own, a few babies with big gray eyes and easy smiles, but I don't say that to her. She's not ready to hear that yet. She's still skittish, and if I push too hard, I think she'll run. I can play the long game.

"I've never gone camping," I answer.

"I had one foster family that took me camping once. We stayed in Oklahoma though."

"Were they nice?" I ask as the GPS tells me our turn is half a mile ahead.

"They were," she pauses trying to find the right word, "there. I never felt like part of their family, but I also didn't feel unsafe or unwanted."

Even as the black sheep of my family I always knew I was loved and wanted. Being sent away to boarding school didn't lessen my feelings of belonging. The endless arguments and disappointment from my father still don't.

I pull into a gravel lot next to a field full of rows of pine trees. Families mill around, walking up and down the rows, looking for the perfect tree. We walk hand in hand over to a small shed where several workers are grouped and get a hand saw.

After describing the size we'd need we're directed to walk to the back of the field where the taller, more mature trees are. Clara's nose and cheeks are already turning pink in the blustery wind, but she happily trudges through the snow anyway. We have matching Santa hats on, her idea of course, I can't tell her no even when it makes me look absurd.

She keeps trying to get me to sing Christmas carols, but singing is my limit, so she goes for a solo performance. She's off key and warbly but perfect regardless. I can't hold my smile back as she does a cute as fuck little shimmy while singing "Santa Baby" and winking at me.

"If you keep looking at me like that, I'm going to think you don't find my love of the holidays annoying, Mr. Scrooge." She smiles at me and then looks around us at the group of trees we're standing in.

She zeros in on one and walks around it, inspecting all sides. "This one."

"Are you sure?"

"Yeah, but what did they tell us? About checking the trunk?"

"To make sure it's straight." I push branches aside, looking inside to examine the trunk like I know what I'm doing.

"What do you think?" she asks, peering inside from under my arm.

"I have no idea, but it looks good to me."

"If you think it's good, I'm sure it is." She gives the saw a pointed look. "Do you know how to use that?"

"You know I'm good with my hands," I say with a smirk.

Her cheeks turn a deeper pink. "You are," she agrees.

She holds the trunk steady while I saw the trunk. They said they'd send a cart, but we start carrying it anyway. It's lighter than I thought it would be and we're moving quick. We buy a base and have the tree netted. The employees help me secure the tree to my roof rack and then we're on our way back.

I convinced her we should pick up Steve and that they should spend the weekend with me. So, we stop there and pick him up. While she's getting the cat, I notice three men leave the apartment across from hers. A glimpse inside their apartment shows multiple bunk beds and my mind spirals on the possibilities.

"Do you know your neighbors across the hall?" I ask, trying for casual but my tone must give me away.

"Calm down." She slaps a Ziploc bag of cat food against my chest. "It's a crash pad for pilots. There's seven or eight of them that share it and stay there when they're trying to commute home or there's no flights. They're all harmless."

I grunt but don't say anything. The rickety excuse for a door to her apartment looks like one kick could knock it off the hinges. I don't like the idea of a bunch of men milling around at all hours of the day. Might have to push a little harder to get her on board.

"Ash?" Clara walks into my office twenty minutes before the holiday party is set to begin. "You're still working? The party starts in twenty minutes, we need to leave."

"It's just across the street, isn't it? I need to finish this and get it sent to some of the New York investors." I do a double take when I look up at her.

She's wearing a short red dress, covered in sequins, a wide black belt, red stilettos, and a Santa hat. I've grown used to her weird taste in clothing, and while she often wears skirts and dresses, they never show much leg. The sight of so much of her skin exposed makes me rock fucking hard.

"You're aiming for the naughty list tonight, I see." I push my chair back and pat my desk. "Come bend over here, and I'll join you on it."

"Please." She giggles. "You live on the naughty list based on your grumpy tendencies alone. Let's go."

"Go on over without me. I'll be right behind you."

"Seriously?" She straightens.

"Yes," I answer exasperated. "Finishing this is more important than a party. If I don't take care of business, there will be no reason to celebrate."

I see the hurt flash in her eyes and feel a pang in my chest, but she walks away with a mumbled okay before I can say anything. I'll make it up to her later, I decide as I dive back into work.

When I finally hit send on the email, I realize it's been over an hour.

Fuck.

I flip all the office lights off and race down the stairs. I don't even wait for the light to change before sprinting across the cross walk. A cab honks as it barely misses me. I dash into the venue and look around.

All my employees are talking and drinking, laughing, and dancing. Until they see me, that is. Then their faces fall, and they step out of my way. Voices drop a level or two in volume. It's like I suck all the fun out of the room with my presence.

I push that realization to the side as I continue to look for Clara. My stomach hardens as my eyes finally find her. She's at the bar talking to Taylor. His hand is on her waist, his thumb moving up and down her side and something inside me snaps.

If I thought everyone was nervous around me before, now they're terrified. The crowd parts for me, allowing me to reach her in seconds and pry her from his hands. Her lips part when she looks at me but not in desire, in anger.

"I need to talk to you, Sunshine." My fingers wrap gently but firmly around her bicep and tug her away from him.

"I'm off the clock, Mr. Bennett. I'm sure whatever you need can wait until tomorrow." She yanks her arm from my hand and turns back to Taylor.

"It's urgent."

"This is a party." She waves her hand around. "Go mingle. Or go back to work, everyone was enjoying their night until you came in to ruin it."

At this point Taylor is looking back and forth between us, trying to figure out what is going on. No one speaks to me like that. She's the exception. She can because I disappointed her, I made her feel unimportant.

"I really must insist."

"She said no." Taylor inserts himself between her and I.

"Leave," I command.

"No." He holds his ground.

"Leave us, or I will fire you and make sure you never set foot in another office anywhere in Chicago. I will blacklist your ass from every tech company from Singapore to Silicon Valley."

"Just go," Clara tells him with an eye roll. "I'll be fine."

He hesitates, brave but stupid. I'm not bluffing.

As soon as he turns, I grab her hand and pull her along behind me until I find an empty bathroom. I flip the lock behind me and turn her to look at me. Her eyes are red-rimmed and just the slightest bit puffy, like she's on the verge of crying, and my chest splits wide open. I put that hurt look on her face.

"I'm so sorry."

"Nothing to be sorry for," she says as a single tear escapes and rolls down her cheek. "It was a good reminder that this isn't anything beyond sex. Just scratching an itch."

"Bullshit," I say with a raised voice. "This is so much more, and you know it."

She chuckles bitterly and shakes her head. "Is it?"

"I've done everything you ask of me. I volunteered with you. I let you plan this party. I bought a Christmas tree with you."

"The funny thing about all that? I just wanted to spend time with you. Anyway I could weasel it out of you. Half the nights I spend with you, you leave me after we fuck to go back to work. And tonight, you couldn't even walk me over to the party. Then you get mad and threaten one of your best employees?" She turns away and angrily swipes a tear from her cheek. "What's even the point of this? We should just end it now, before it gets messier."

"No." I step behind her, pressing her into the counter and meeting her eyes in the mirror. "We're not ending it."

"Why?"

"Because I love you."

CHAPTER 21

CLARA

MY HEART SOARS, even as my stomach drops. He just told me he loves me. Asher Bennett loves me, the eccentric orphan from Oklahoma with nothing but a shitty apartment and a cat to her name. He drops his forehead to my shoulder and squeezes my waist.

"I'm so in love with you that half the time I can't concentrate on anything except you. My heart races every time you enter a room. I know you're scared, but so am I. Let's be scared together."

He drops to his knees behind me, running his hands up the back of my legs and pushing my skirt up over my hips.

"What are you doing?" I ask as he peels my panties down my legs, lifting one out of them.

"I'm going to eat this pussy until you scream my name and beg for my cock."

"People will hear us." I draw a quick breath when his finger finds my clit, brushing it tantalizingly slowly.

"Good." He pushes down on my back, flattening me against the counter and putting myself on full display for him. "Let them."

He parts my folds with his thumbs, opening me for him completely as he licks me with the flat of his tongue from my clit to my entrance. I arch back against his mouth as he plays with me, alternating between laving my clit and fucking me with his tongue.

I feel my orgasm building deep within my core and he's right, I am about to beg for his cock. All I want is to feel him filling me, stretching me, owning me. His lips wrap around my tiny bud as he plunges two fingers inside me, curling them to hit my g-spot.

"Ash," I gasp his name. "I'm going to come."

I feel him smile against me as he continues his delicious assault on my body. He reaches up with his free hand and pulls the zipper on my dress down, then unhooks my bra.

The orgasm rips through me like a hot tidal wave. I have to bite down on my lip to keep from crying out through the waves of pleasure. He laps at me until the final tremors fade and then he stands. He gives me a devilish grin, his lips glistening with my release as he pulls the straps of my dress down, freeing my breasts. He reaches around, kneading them softly as he kisses my neck and presses his cock, straining against his pants, against me.

He turns me around and hitches me up on the counter, stepping between my legs as he unzips his pants. He pulls his cock out and runs it along my seam, making both of us inhale with the pleasure of his skin pressed against mine.

"Watch me." He presses his crown against my entrance. "Watch me own you."

His lips slam against mine in a desperate, wild clash of need. I taste myself on him as our tongues slide against each other. I nip his lip, causing him to growl against me as he pushes inside of me. His hand slides into my hair and tilts my head down so I can watch him sheathed within me.

"Mine," he says as he glides back in. "Mine."

Over and over, he chants it, as if he's hammering his claim into me. My hips arch to meet his every stroke. Nothing has ever felt as good as he does. I doubt anything ever will.

He lifts me from the counter, his hands holding me by the bottoms of my thighs and presses me against the wall. His cock drills into me, over and over, our rhythm pounding against the wall. I wrap my legs around his waist as I spasm around him, my pussy milking the release from his cock.

He rests his forehead against mine as he spills inside me and doesn't pull out until both of us catch our breath. We smile at each other with heaving chests as my feet hit the floor. He tucks himself back into his pants and then kneels in front of me.

"Thank you," I tell him as he helps me back into my panties properly.

"No, thank you." He pauses before pulling them over

my knees. I look down, puzzled as to why he would stop. Then I realize what he's doing as his fingers run along the inside of my thighs, gathering his cum that's run down my legs. He pushes his fingers, coated in his cum, up and inside me. Afterward, he pulls my panties up the rest of the way and kisses my mound. "I love that we're going back out there with my cum dripping from your pussy."

"Everyone is going to know."

He hums in agreement.

"Aren't you worried?" I ask as I refasten my bra.

"No." He spins me around and zips my dress back up.

"Really? Even though I'm your employee?"

"Are you planning on filing a lawsuit? Do you feel coerced into this relationship?"

"No."

"Good." He adjusts his cuffs and tie. "Your opinion is the only one I care about. Are you ready for everyone to know?"

"I think it's too late now, even if I wasn't." They all probably heard me crying out his name five minutes ago. I slide my hand into his. "Let's do this."

Thankfully Nico and Stella are at the other end of the building giving toasts when we walk out of the bathroom. Most eyes are turned to them as Nico makes jokes and Stella rolls her eyes. All except Taylor, who looks at me with a shuttered and disappointed expression.

Ash notices and steps between us, breaking my line of sight. He pulls me close, and I wrap my arms around his waist. Nico makes a joke about him and calls him up to say a few words. I watch as he smiles at his employees grouped around the room. He thanks everyone for such a great year and asserts that next year is going to be even better. Then his eyes land on me, and I know he's going to say something, bring some sort of attention to me.

"I know you all know this party wouldn't have happened without Clara. In such a short time with TechJet, she's brought so much to the table." A few murmured jokes and laughter reach my ears but not his. "Let's give her a round of applause for all her hard work."

My cheeks heat as everyone turns to look at me, so I keep my eyes on Ash as he looks down at me with nothing but pride in his gaze. A hand lands on my back, and I turn to a smiling Taylor.

"Congratulations. I didn't take you for a gold digger, but you landed a fat wallet." His smile never fades, even as he delivers the words laced with venom.

Stella notices the interaction and starts to move toward us, but Taylor disappears out the front door before she can reach us either. She comes over to me with concern on her face.

"What did he say?" she asks.

"Nothing." I shrug off her concern. "Everything is fine."

"Bullshit. All the color drained from your face."

"Listen. Yeah, he said something rude, but I'll have to get used to it if I'm dating Ash. He's wealthy, gorgeous, smart, and there's not a woman in the city who wouldn't date him without a second thought. I'm just a temp."

"First of all, there is a woman in this city who wouldn't

date him, and you're looking at her. Second of all, yes, people will talk, but that doesn't excuse someone who knows you from being an asshole. Last and most important, you are not just a temp. You are gorgeous, intelligent, funny, and warm. If anyone is punching up, it's Ash, not you."

"He's coming over, don't say anything to him. He already threatened Taylor's job earlier."

"What's wrong?" he asks as soon as he joins us, Nico right behind him.

"Nothing, just girl talk." Stella takes his hand. "Dance with me and take the heat off Clara."

"Are you okay, Sunshine?" he asks, firmly planted in front of me as Stella pulls him in the opposite direction. His deep green eyes surveying me up and down as if I've been in a physical altercation.

"Yes, I'm fine. Go dance." I say as I shoo him away.

"It's okay," Nico places his hand on my back and guides me onto the dance floor. "My turn to dance with her."

Nico sweeps me out into the crowd and pulls me into his arms. He laughs at the scowl on Asher's face and pulls me just a bit closer.

"You're bad," I say with a laugh.

"He's ridiculous." He smiles down at me. "You make him happy."

"I hope so."

"Does he do the same?"

"He does." Most of the time anyway, but I'm not going to say that to his best friend.

"If he ever doesn't, tell him. Give him a chance to fix it.

He's driven and focused, always has been. It's how he's gotten so far in life, but it gives him tunnel vision. I don't want to watch him lose you because he can't multitask."

The air feels heavy between us after that, even with Nico dipping me and reverting back to light-hearted jokes. Maybe it's the lingering hurt after being left on my own at the beginning of the party that has soured the whole experience. It could be the doubts pin balling around my mind after Taylor's comments, too. I just don't know.

CHAPTER 22

ASHER

CLARA HASN'T BEEN the same since the party. Her eyes lack their usual luster as she moves throughout the mundane activities of life. I want to know what Taylor said to her, but every time I've brought it up, she evades. When my parents invited me to dinner and I told them I'd be bringing my girlfriend, I had hoped everything would be back to normal.

Father said he had some important business opportunity to bring to my attention. He's been trying for years to get me involved in the family business. I turn him down every time and then the tension between us all increases. I don't want Clara walking into that volatility unprepared, but I don't want her scared, either.

She's quiet as we ride to my parents' estate out in the

suburbs, her hand tucked into mine and her clothing elegant and understated. I kind of wish she had on one of her ugly Christmas sweaters though, with cookie leggings or something. She shines when she opens the curtains and gives the world a glimpse of her soul. Dressing in a black wrap dress is like boarding the windows.

"Which of your brothers will be there?" she asks quietly.

"Trent and his wife Christine, maybe their daughters, Tilly and Maggie. Henry will probably be there as well. Ian is out of the country with his family." I reach over and grab her hand, pulling it into my lap. "Are we okay?"

She turns her head, looking down at our linked hands before looking up at me. "Yeah, I'm just nervous. I've never met a boyfriend's family. Our introduction at the gala was so brief, I doubt they even remember my name."

"Honestly, they probably don't, but that's not a bad thing. Just stay close to me and remember that their opinion doesn't matter at the end of the day. I love you, and that's all that matters."

It still stings that she hasn't said I love you back yet, but I'd rather her know for sure than lie and leave me someday. Not that I plan on letting her walk away. I already have a timeline in my mind of how this relationship will transgress with three to five months leeway for each stage.

The whole cliché of 'you just know when you know' always felt phony to me, but now I get it. I think I knew the second she walked in on me changing. The way her eyes locked on mine, and I was embarrassed but intrigued. I've wanted more of her every second since.

As soon as the car comes to a stop the front door of my parents' home swings open. Their butler opens the car door for Clara and helps her out. I come around and guide her up the granite steps and past the imposing columns on the front porch.

Mother is standing in the foyer, wearing a blue dress and her signature pearls. Her graying hair is swept back in a twist, as always. She steps forward and reintroduces herself to Clara. I watch the encounter with a keen eye, making sure she doesn't get any jabs in. She still makes backhanded comments to Christine, and she's been married to Trent for twelve years.

"Shall we?" I ask Mother as I gently lead Clara past her and into the living room where they entertain guests before a meal.

The room hasn't changed since I was a boy. It is traditional in design with dark, masculine colors and uncomfortable furniture. Weird, overpriced art adorns the walls. I always preferred to spend my free time in the backyard or library. But luckily, I was rarely home, so I didn't have to deal with the formality of entertaining with them.

"Father, you remember Clara." We find him pouring a glass of scotch from a crystal decanter.

He turns and gives her a lecherous look. "The assistant, right?"

She shakes his offered hand. "Yes, temporary assistant."

"Making good use of it, I see." He turns to me, effectively dismissing her. "I need to go over a few things with you in the study before dinner."

I nod and turn to Clara, squeezing her bicep. "I'll be right back. If Trent and Christine show up, stick close to her."

"Okay." She brushes her lips across mine, but it's not enough. I deepen the kiss and give her lower lip a quick nibble. She blushes and smiles at me as I follow my dad out of the room.

"Son, clearly I went wrong with you at some point. Assistants are for fucking and getting your laundry from the cleaners."

My stomach turns at the way he talks about women.

"You need a woman who can carry herself well and look good on your arm. Maybe pop out a few kids to keep the family name alive." He sets a pile of papers down in front of me. "Sign these, and we can get dinner over with."

"What is it?" I start to read, seeing they are real estate contracts of some sort.

"I need to use your trust holdings as collateral for an offer on a block I'm trying to buy up on the south side."

I almost ask why he's looking down there, but decide I don't care. I decided a long time ago I would never use the trust from him for anything. The last thing I want is his nasty money infiltrating my company and dirtying up Tech-Jet's reputation. So I scrawl my name next to all the arrows and leave him to it.

When I walk into the dining room, I find Clara and Christine talking quietly while Mother speaks to Trent.

Unfortunately for me, my nieces are nowhere to be found. Those two are the only thing that makes these dinners bearable.

"Christine." I lean down and kiss her cheek in greeting. "Where are the girls?"

"At my parents' house this weekend."

We sit and chat until Trent walks over for an introduction. Clara is finally warming up and letting her personality shine through when my father walks back in, dragging the dark cloud that follows him everywhere. He's wearing a smug smirk as he sits down, and the food is brought out.

Everyone minds their manners but under the facade of civility are little barbs aimed at both Christine and Clara. Everything from comments about the charity Christine is on the board of to remarks about high society decorum. I hold Clara's hand under the table and redirect my mother's attention.

Clara excuses herself to use the restroom and Mother takes the opportunity to pounce.

"Asher, I know you think that the rules don't apply to you since you left the family business but that's just not true." She dabs her mouth with her napkin.

"The rules don't apply to me because they're bullshit, Mother."

"She's beneath you in station."

"This isn't the Regency era." I scoff and lean back in my chair. "There are no stations in life."

"Yes, there are. You are a member of a family with over

a billion-dollar net worth. You cannot be serious about dating an orphan."

"Mother," I hold a hand up to stop her.

"Don't 'Mother' me, Asher. Did you ever stop to figure out why no one wanted her? Do you really want her possible defects passed onto your children?"

"No one wanted me because I was labeled a high-needs baby. My mother was a sex worker who died of an overdose after being clean for most of her pregnancy and my first year of life," Clara says from the door. Her back is straight, and she regards my mother with a mirrored, cold look. "As for any possible genetic issues, I'm quite healthy and, dare I say, bright. I got a full ride to Northwestern where I got my MBA in three years. I choose to be a temp, but I assure you, I could be anything I wanted."

"So you have no ambition." Father sneers from the end of the table. "You waste all that work and intelligence making minimum wage when you could have so much more."

"I'm very fulfilled, actually."

"Yeah, by my son's cock and his money."

"Stop." I stand and glare at my parents. "I will not have you speak to the woman I love like that. Consider this our last family meal. I'm done."

I usher her out as my mom tries to stop us with half-hearted apologies. I open the car door for Clara and close it behind her before whirling on my mother. Blood is pounding through my veins so hard that my ears are ringing.

"How dare you, Mother? How fucking dare you? I

knew you were shallow, but I didn't realize you were cruel as well. When I marry that woman," I gesture behind me into the car, "you will not be in attendance. You won't even know it happened until it is announced in the papers. I will marry her because she is warm, and funny, and smart. Everything you should want for your child when it comes time to pick their partner."

Her eyes start to water as I continue yelling. I'm too incensed to care. She could fill Lake Michigan with her tears and I wouldn't so much as hand her a tissue.

"Tell you what, since you care so much about appearances, I'll send you some photographs of my stunning bride and myself as we say our vows."

I get in the car and slam the door. Luckily Tom floors it, and we're out of the neighborhood in no time. My jaw aches with tension as I study Clara's profile. She's pale and withdrawn again. I reach over for her hand, but she moves away from me.

"This isn't going to work," she says quietly. "I don't think we should see each other anymore."

"No." I move over and wrap my arm around her. "I know my parents were awful, but we'll never see them again."

"You can't pick me over your family. Don't put me in that position, to be the reason you become like me, with no family, no ties. I could never live with myself if you did that."

"It isn't your fault. It's theirs. They were the assholes."

"It doesn't matter." She reaches up and touches Tom's

shoulder. "Take me home after you drop Mr. Bennett off, please."

I start seeing spots as my world fractures around me. She's all I want. I struggle to take a breath as the lights of Chicago grow brighter around us. Her face and her voice are so serene as she sits there. How is she doing this? How is she so calm and rational as our foundation rattles to its destruction?

"Sunshine, you're hurting. You don't mean this."

"I do." She turns to me and squeezes my hand. "This was always just a fantasy. We're from such different worlds. I don't belong in yours."

"Fuck my world and the people in it."

"Let me go. It's better this way."

"I love you," the words come out hoarse.

"You love the idea of me," she answers without looking at me.

Tom's face is pained when he opens the door for me. I barely focus on walking inside my building and finding the right elevator. By the time I get to my apartment, I'm numb and looking for a way to get even more numb. I go straight to my liquor cabinet and grab the first thing I see, a bottle of bourbon. I flick the cap off and chug straight from the bottle. It dulls the pain, but it doesn't remove the scent of orange and vanilla from my sheets when I finally pass out.

CHAPTER 23

CLARA

AS SOON AS I see Asher walk into his building the sobs I've been trying so hard to hold back erupt from my chest. It feels like someone reached into my chest and ripped my heart out. I love him. I love him so much it terrifies me.

I love him too much to let him push his family away on my behalf. I cannot be the reason he becomes estranged and disinherited. Not when he has family, however dysfunctional they are. However cruel they can be.

The tears and sobs don't stop the entire drive to my apartment. Tom opens the car door and starts to say something but just pulls me to him in a hug that I didn't realize I needed. He holds me while I cry until someone honks because he's double parked.

After murmured goodbyes, I walk up to my tiny, lonely

apartment. At least Steve wasn't at Asher's tonight. I don't think I could make it through this without him, even if he ignores me. I lock the door behind me and collapse onto the bed, giving into the tears.

The day after our break was grim. I called the temp agency and claimed I had a family emergency. I told them I wouldn't be able to finish my term at TechJet, and they sent word to the company on my behalf. The thought of walking into the office to get my meager belongs turned my stomach so I just let it go.

I know I wouldn't be able to handle seeing him. I would cave. I would drop to my knees and beg him to take me back. Every hour without him has been excruciating. I haven't even showered because I can still faintly smell his cologne on my skin, and it's been three days.

I'm halfway through a Netflix binge when I hear a knock on my door. I stand up and open the door without looking. I open my door to see Nico and Stella standing on the other side of the threshold. Nico is holding a box with my belongings, and Stella is holding an iced coffee and a box of donuts.

"You look like shit," Nico says as he steps inside. "Nearly as bad Ash." He looks around, looking for a place to put the box down and settles with the floor.

"Peace offering." Stella hands me the donuts and coffee. "How are you doing?"

"I'm fine, thank you."

"Lies. This place looks like a tornado tore through. And those bags under your eyes are bigger than a carry on." Nico pushes the blanket on my bed to the side and sits down.

"If you're going to be a dick, I'm sending you back out to wait with Tom," Stella tells him.

He holds his hands up in a peace gesture.

"Did you get a new temp? Are they doing well?" I ask, determined to keep the conversation on work and not Asher.

"The temp is fine, old and cranky but competent," Nico says.

"Yes, now we have a Scrooge and grump. They feed off each other," Stella adds.

"Asher isn't good. He misses you." They share a look. "We've never seen him this bad."

"He's better off without me. Just bringing me to a family dinner caused enough strife to last a decade. I don't want that for him."

"Doesn't what he wants count for something?" Stella asks. "He wants you."

"Over his family," Nico adds.

"That's the thing, though." I remember I'm holding a box of donuts and set it aside. "It shouldn't be one or the other."

"Give him another chance," Stella begs.

"He loves you."

"I love him, too. I just don't want to be the reason a family fractures."

They share another look before turning their attention to me. "You love him?"

I feel the blood drain from my face. That admission just slipped out. "Don't tell him."

They share another look and I swear I can feel them mentally conversing.

"We won't tell him."

"That should be on you."

"But," Nico holds up a hand, "you have to swear to hear him out if he approaches you."

"Is he planning on doing so?"

Nico shrugs. Stella looks over my shoulder. Then her phone rings, and she glances down. "Fuck, I need to take this." She looks up at me apologetically. "I'll come back with a of bottle wine, soon, okay?"

"Yeah, that actually sounds great." It does. I never notice how alone I am until there's no one there in the dark moments.

They both hug me, and I go back to binging the latest Netflix craze.

CHAPTER 24

ASHER

MY LEG BOUNCES with nerves as I wait for the committeeman to open his door. Everything I'm about to do is wildly risky, but there's two driving factors. One, it's the right thing to do. Two, it'll make Clara happy.

When my personal real estate attorney reached out to me two days ago about finalizing numbers for the block on the south side, I was floored. I had completely forgotten about signing those papers. Luckily, everyone on my team knows to double and triple check with me when any of my business, be it private or corporate, is mixed up with my father's.

When he sent me the paperwork, I could hardly believe it, my father was trying to buy the entire block that the shelter Clara volunteers at sits on. He wanted to push them off and build a strip mall, more than likely to be filled with predatory businesses like payday loans.

It took almost two days straight of going back and forth with attorneys and bankers and brokers before I finally was approved to buy the land out from under my father. Since he was using my trust as collateral, I was able to just fund the entire purchase outright, and if I can convince the committeeman to help with the zoning changes, the deed will be in the shelter's name by end of business Monday.

I'm finally called in and sit across from the bored looking man. After fawning over my family name and asking about my father, he listens as I give the most impassioned speech I've ever delivered on why the zoning needs to change and the vision I have for the shelter. How it could bring life to what is currently a blighted area.

I'm just finishing up my conversation with him when his secretary calls to let him know Daniel and Clara are here. He assumes they know I'm here and tells her to let them in.

Daniel walks in first and does a double take upon seeing me. He steps aside, and Clara walks in, digging through a bag and not looking at me. She's thinner than she was days ago, and when her eyes meet mine, I see what Nico was talking about. She has dark circles under those gorgeous gray eyes of hers, and every fiber of my being wants to go erase them.

"Ash," she says, stunned. "I didn't think you'd remember."

"How could I forget?" I want to stride across the room

and sweep her into my arms. I want to press her against the wall and remind her how good we are together. How she's my home and I'm hers. But I hold myself back.

The committeeman stands and gestures for both to take a seat. "I have good news." He looks at me. "Mr. Bennett has purchased the other part of the block and will be donating it to the shelter. With everything that he outlined for me, I don't think there should be any problem getting the zoning changed for you."

"That is," Daniel pauses to let it soak in, "absolutely incredible." He stands and holds out his hand to me. "Thank you so much, Mr. Bennett. I truly have no words."

"My pleasure. What you are doing there is so good, so important. This is really the least I could do. Someone once told me that you can't just throw money at problems, but in this case I think it's okay."

"In this case it is absolutely okay," he turns to Clara and hugs her as she cries.

Her eyes dart to me, wet with tears as she gives me a tremulous smile.

They start lobbing questions back and forth, none directed at me, so I stand and quietly make my way out of the office. I'm glad I could put that smile on her face, even if I only got to see it once more.

My world is so bleak without her. I'll hold onto that moment in there for a long time to come. Part of me screams to go back, to throw her over my shoulder and take her home. I seriously consider kidnapping her for a minute, but

I know, if she's going to come back to me, it has to be of her own free will.

I push the lobby door open and step out into the blustery cold Chicago wind. Snow is falling, picture perfect for Christmas Eve. I gave Tom the last ten days of December off, so I start walking toward my apartment. It's only about ten blocks, not worth the hassle of a cab on a holiday. Plus, I don't have anywhere to be.

I turned down all invitations. I blocked all numbers my parents have. Trent was so disgusted by our parents' behavior that he and Christine took the girls on a surprise ski trip to Aspen. He invited me, but I declined. Seeing my brother and his wife, happy and in love as a family, feels too raw right now.

"Ash!"

I pause, scared that I was hearing things I wanted to hear, not that are real. I don't want to turn around and realize it was a figment of my imagination. Then I feel her hand on my back.

"Ash," she says softly. "Turn around."

I do, and when our eyes meet, I watch as hers overflow with tears. I can't stop myself from cupping her cheek and wiping them with my thumb. "Are these happy or sad tears, Sunshine?"

"Both?" she hiccups with a sob. "I don't know how to thank you. I don't...I'm speechless."

"You don't have to thank me. Ever." I knew being close to her again would hurt, but I didn't expect the torrent of longing and love to be so overpowering. "Just be happy."

I turn to walk away because I'm going to break if I don't.

"I'm not," she calls to my back. "I'm not happy without you. Don't make me say it to your back."

"Say what?" I ask as I turn to face her.

"That I love you. That I've loved you since the beginning, even when you'd give me shit about decorating for Christmas before Thanksgiving. When you would roll your eyes at my ugly Christmas sweaters. I loved you when you protected me. I loved you beneath the Eiffel Tower. I loved you then, and I still love you now. I was just too scared to admit it."

The world stops around us as we look into each other's souls. If I touch her now, it's the end. We're together, forever.

"If I come to you, I'm never letting you go. You realize that, right? I will literally handcuff you to my bed."

She starts to walk to me. "That sounds promising."

I walk toward her, our speed increasing until we're wrapped in each other's arms again. Nothing has ever felt as right as when our lips finally meet again. The kiss is fervent and needy, sloppy, and entirely too public but I don't give a fuck. She moans into my mouth, pulling a groan from me. We stand there, kissing in the snow on a cold, gray December day, and life has never made more sense.

"I have one question," she says as she breaks our kiss. "Do you have any chicken nuggets?"

EPILOGUE

CLARA
EIGHT MONTHS LATER

I NEVER THOUGHT my life would end up like this. Ash moved me into his place immediately, which made Steve incredibly happy. He roams around the large penthouse like a lazy king.

Daniel offered me a full time position working at the shelter, which I happily accepted. With the donations that Asher has helped us secure we've planned out a small village of tiny homes and an expansion to the current shelter, including a large gymnasium and refurbished bathroom facilities.

Ash suggested we look into hiring Jack, who he has become close to over the months, to head the construction effort. He's living in the tiny home prototype that was recently completed. I was surprised at how fast it went up and how for a small space, it feels roomy. The best part is seeing how Jack is thriving with this new job and direction in his life. I love watching the relationship the two of them have developed.

"You look gorgeous," Ash says as he stands behind me in the bathroom. "I knew this dress would be perfect."

I look down at the hunter green dress I'm wearing for the ribbon cutting today. Every few months Stella drags me out to go shopping. More often than not I've found that she takes photos and sends them to Ash in case there's a dress that looks amazing but I can't bring myself to buy. This is one of them.

I turn to face him. He's wearing a navy suit sans tie with the top buttons of his shirt undone. Straight up suit porn. I'm considering jumping him when he lowers to one knee.

At first I think he's just tying his shoe but then he looks up, a little blue box in his hand. Everything inside me seizes with anticipation when his glassy eyes find mine.

"Clara Snow, you have made the last year of my life the brightest and warmest. I didn't realize I could love so deeply and fully until you walked into my office. I think, on some level, I knew as soon as I saw you that you were the one. You make me a better man."

He opens the box, revealing a pear shaped diamond ring with smaller diamonds set into the band on either side. It's gorgeous while still being understated.

"Will you marry me?" he asks.

"Yes," I say as I drop to my knees and kiss him with tears streaming down my face. "I love you so much."

"I love you, too."

You'll get to see more of Clara and Ash's happy ending in Nico and Stella's story.

Coming during the 2023 holiday season.

ACKNOWLEDGEMENTS

I'm going to keep it short and sweet for this one. I have to thank my family first and foremost. Your never-ending understanding for when I disappear for hours to write is something I could never adequately expressive my gratitude for.

Miranda and Chloe, I love you both in equal measure. You keep sane when nothing else helps.

Victoria, thank you so much for always working with me. I know it's probably super irritating to work around my chronic illness and I will sing your praises for all time.

Cassie, you knocked this cover out of the park. It was literally everything I had envisioned but a hundred times better.

Brianna, THANK YOU SO MUCH for always matching energy with me, especially for this holiday sexiness.

My street team, I wouldn't be without your support. You all are so dear to me.

My beta team, Val, Sherry, Jennifer, and Ash. Thank you so much for reading and providing feedback. Your thoughts and suggestions are invaluable.

STALK ME HERE

www.nicholegreenebooks.com

Instagram: @nicholegreene.author

Tiktok: @nicholegreeneauthor

Facebook: https://www.facebook.com/nicholegreeneauthor

Reader Group: https://www.facebook.com/groups/213086921000006548

Goodreads: https://www.goodreads.com/author/show/20181440.Nichole_Greene

Amazon: https://www.amazon.com/Nichole-Greene/e/B0854B1MJB/ref=dp_byline_cont_pop_ebooks_1

ALSO BY NICHOLE GREENE

STANDALONES

Seven Days

The Hunt

Dark Devotions

Painted in the Shadows *coming December 26, 2022*

TWISTED LEGACIES SERIES

Savage Love

Reckless Love

Sinful Love *coming Winter 2023*

Printed in Great Britain
by Amazon

31646683R00108